Warrant for Damnation

Warrant for Damnation

ANGELS DARK AND DUMB
BOOK 2

Winnie Jean Howard

www.winniejeanhoward.com

ARMLIN HOUSE PRODUCTIONS

Warrant for Damnation

Copyright © 2023 by Winnie Jean Howard

Cover Artwork Copyright © 2023 by Rebecca Treadway

ArmLin House Productions
P.O. Box 2522, Littleton, Colorado 80161-2522

ISBN: 978-1-958185-07-0

Cover Design by Atrtink Covers
www.atrtinkcovers.com

Printed in the United States of America

First Edition

Always for Michael
My Heart
My Inspiration

Chapter 1

WHO IN his right mind goes home with a stranger he met on the highway like I did last night? Then again, it's not the stupidest thing I've done over the past four days.

I peek outside the bedroom where I've tossed and turned the last few hours. At nearly five in the morning, the second-floor hallway is deserted. Perfect for a speedy getaway. But there's no telling who or what lurks behind the oak doors that break up the flowery red-and-gold wallpaper.

On an ordinary workday, I'd rush off to my courier job for Hell. Yes, the literal Hell. Then I'd spend half my day pissing off my demon boss Margery, although not on purpose.

No work today though. As of yesterday, life is…*complicated*.

While I'm innocent, Margery managed to convince Satan that I sabotaged his plan to open the Gates of Hell. And God believes I sacrificed hundreds of His white warriors to get the job done. Worst of all, Margery's Minotaurs took off with my friend Nina before we were able to escape together.

Floorboards creak under my skater shoes as I duck into the hallway, my messy brown curls brushing under the doorframe. The smell of pancakes rises from the first floor and awakens my senses in a bad way. Fruity flavored cereal and gin are more my breakfast of champions, but it doesn't matter. No time to eat. I've got to sneak out and save Nina from the seven levels of misery that Margery's likely inflicting on her.

A doorknob clicks to my left.

Damn!

Pete exits a bedroom with a smile. "Morning, Barry. Able to sleep?"

He's the stranger who brought me to this old farmhouse, and he'll try to convince me to stay. Pete professes to be a miracle worker for the Catholic Church and can smooth things over with God. He's also promised to nullify my contract with Satan and provide protection against Hell's bounty hunters. Boy, I want to believe him, but the mosh pit of butterflies in my stomach warn to trust no one.

My grip tightens on the wood-carved railing. *Get out. Find Nina.*

On impulse, my feet take off, descending the stairs at hyper-speed, as if I'm *The Flash* in the comic book series. Unable to control this ability attained during a trip to Hell's refugee camp, all I can do is tuck and go into a double somersault to put on the brakes. I land on something rigid at the bottom of the staircase, pain erupting in my ribs.

"Damn!" I shiver at the sight of a wooden shard from the broken coat rack piercing my t-shirt and torso at my side. I grit my teeth, grab the protruding spike, and yank. Cupping the gash is no help. Bright red blood oozes between my fingers and drips onto my baggy jeans.

Seems everything I do lately turns to shit or a fountain of gore.

Pete descends to the first floor, my body twitching with each heavy step of his cowboy boots. He's more wrinkled than I remember. Maybe his jet-black pompadour concealed his age.

He sweeps back his tan tweed jacket and slides a thumb into the front pocket of his jeans. The way he dresses, the guy could be a cowboy professor.

"I'd ask how you feel," he says, "but that wound is answer enough."

While struggling to pick up my glasses and stand on unsteady legs, I clench my jaw tighter and suck air between my teeth.

"Hold on, Barry." Pete skips down the last few steps. "Let me help."

Still clutching my ribs, I recoil, suspicious of anything he's offering. "It'll heal in a few minutes."

"Let's at least get you tidied up," he says, "and into clean clothes."

"Thanks, but no time." I face the front door, decorated with panes of yellow-stained glass. "Besides, I shouldn't be here. I have to find Nina before Margery turns her into a demon chew toy." My gaze drops, knowing what a gutless loser I am for leaving her behind.

"Two seconds outside and you'll have Hell's bounty hunters fighting to take you in for closing the hellhole. At least stick around long enough to break your contract with Satan. They won't be able to track you."

"You saw me move. I'm too fast to catch."

"But not very coordinated." He lifts an eyebrow and half grins.

After a brief pause, I sidestep toward the door.

"Nina's fine." Pete pulls a cell phone from his blazer pocket. "Oscar's keeping an eye on her at the warehouse. Call him. He'll let you talk to her."

"He hates me, not to mention he's Margery's lackey."

"Like I told you. Oscar's a double agent. He's been feeding me information for years and has always been reliable." Pete waves the phone. "Go ahead. His number's the last incoming call."

I blow out a long sigh, reach for the cell, and grasp it with blood-soaked fingers. Instead of contacting Oscar, I flip through the call log and find the names of people close to me. I glare at Pete, feeling more guarded than ever. "Why've you been talking to my mother and Father Timothy?"

"She's worried…" he stutters. "They're worried, Barry, and I've been watching—"

"Watching Margery take my soul and turn me into a wanted man."

"Remember last night, when I mentioned Margery blamed me for closing the Gates of Hell the year you were born? I understand what you're going through. It's why you should stay. Barry, please, there's so much more you need to know."

The phone slips out of my hand and falls to the floor. My only thought, *No one can be trusted, not even Mom.*

I'm out the door at hyper-speed, my side erupting with pain.

Chapter 2

No surprise, my speedy feet take me to the deserted break area outside Margery's Southern Colorado warehouse. They have a way of knowing where I need to be, so it's a given that Nina's nearby.

I drop to my knees and barf stomach acid across the patio: a thing that happens after a run, brought on by strobing lights and absolute terror during a trip. Then again, being this close to my demon boss is equally sickening. Whatever the cause, I'll never get used to it.

I wipe my mouth with the back of my hand. Saliva trails to where I rub the string off on my jeans, inches below my crusted wound. As much as my torso still burns, I'm more focused on Nina. She's probably inside, massaging Margery's smelly feet and splintered toenails. The thought makes the nausea linger.

The dawn glows in the sky, and a cool summer breeze sweeps through the trees and over my arms, raising the hairs. Then the sight of two vintage soda machines against the rusty warehouse wall sends the chill along my spine. If only they'd serve a cold drink to wash away the nasty coating on my tongue. Instead, they dispense the spiny essence of a demon through a direct connect to Hell. The very ones Margery uses to possess and control her workers.

While I escaped that fate, Nina did not. A reminder the demon that possesses her may be an obstacle to leaving this place.

Off to the left, a tall figure in red coveralls rounds the corner, approaches a broken picnic table, and brushes against sunflowers that grow between cracks in the concrete. A salt-and-pepper braid rests near a nametag that reads "Oscar."

When he sees me, his high cheekbones, brown weathered complexion, and turned-down mouth express his usual stoic mood and equal irritation that I'm here.

"You gonna tattle to Pete?" I sneer at him, annoyed that Oscar's a double agent for good and evil. But I'm also relieved he's not Margery.

He removes a flip phone from his pocket, and in a deep, monotone voice says, "While I would enjoy seeing you suffer at the hands of Margery, I will tattle to Pete, as you say."

"Where's Nina?" I step toward him, but my foot catches on a crack, driving me headfirst into his jutted chest. It's like head butting a light pole.

"If it were not for Pete, I would launch you to the moon." Oscar's way of reminding me there's only one thing upon which we agree. We hate each other.

I straighten my bloody shirt, step close to his face, and burp the words, "Where is she?" Considering he's nearly tall enough to look me straight in the eye, he got a full dose of my sour breath.

"Such a fool. You cannot win this contest." His expression contorts as he releases a loud fart.

"What did you eat?" I fan searing nostrils.

"Fermented eggs." Oscar pulls a plastic bag from his pocket. Inside, the putrid snack has been bitten through to a black yolk. "Counteracts Margery's diarrhea curse when she is unsatisfied with my work. Want one?"

"Hell no." After the tortures I've witnessed the evil bitch inflict upon him, he'll need at least a dozen after Nina and I escape.

"Suit yourself." Oscar shoves the bag into his pocket, speed-dials the flip phone, and places it beside his ear. A few seconds later, he says, "Yes, Pete, the fool has arrived."

I yank away the antiquated cell. "Call off your mole. I'm not leaving without Nina."

"Fine." The line goes silent. "Bring her back to the boarding house. We'll protect you both."

Having no actual plan on where to take Nina, his offer is tempting. And we're better off with him than anywhere else. "Full disclosure on everything?"

"That was my intent before you left," he says. "It's time you know about your father, your birth, your purpose."

Oscar turns his attention to where he entered, then lifts his chin and sniffs the air.

My stomach drops as I pull the phone away from my ear. There's no denying that odor.

Cigarette smoke.

Chapter 3

"Look who's here." Margery trounces around the corner wearing an orange Bronco's t-shirt, shiny blue spandex pants, and black flat shoes. She tosses a smoldering butt at Oscar, landing a hex over his heart with an electrical surge.

Oscar's face stiffens, but the tough bastard remains silent, hiding the pain she's inflicted, as he always does. A thing about him I respect.

In a gruff New York accent, Margery asks, "Did I hear Barry right? My most trusted employee is working with Pete?"

I flip the phone closed and slip it into my pocket. This is bad. What will Pete do when he finds out I've exposed his informant? And what else will Margery do to punish Oscar?

Rather than confirm her suspicions, I call out, "If you need to torture someone, torture me."

"Why? You deserve a doggie treat for crawling back to expose this traitor." Margery winks an eye smeared with black liner and turns up an evil grin that exposes nicotine-stained teeth. A few days ago, the sight of her wrinkled mug and flaming troll doll hair made me want to piss my pants. Today, I'm fighting the urge to wring her neck.

"Not a chance I'm crawling back… to you!"

"What other choice do you have, Honey? God and Satan are out to get you." She holds up a hand, magically flips another lit cigarette out of thin air, and explodes into a mixed cackle and emphysema cough.

"Only because of you." I think how stupid I was to fall into her trap. To let her set me up for closing the Gates of Hell.

Two short and scrawny dudes wearing red hoodies and jeans round the building with their heads covered, making them difficult to see in the emerging morning light. Nina's the last to stumble into view. Her long, blond hair dances in the breeze, and her slender body swims in a pair of red coveralls with the sleeves and pant legs rolled up.

I lock onto her violet eyes, a side-effect of being possessed by a demon. When she smiles, my heart races. Thank God she's okay. But when I wave her over, her lips purse and she shakes her head. Must be her demon responding, or more likely she's terrified.

Margery's back on Oscar, flicking successive cigarettes at him like a sharpshooter. "How long have you been helping Pete?" He stumbles backward with each hit but stays on his feet. Her sadistic curse fuses his mouth, and his lips disappear. It's obvious she's not expecting a response. I would know. She's done the same to me.

Oscar's white socks come into view, noticeable as his uniform shrinks in size. Unzipping his suit provides no relief from her next punishment, a full body wedgie.

"Stop it!" Saliva spews from my mouth. This is all my fault, but what can I do?

"Don't worry, Honey." She snorts. "If I hadn't chopped off his balls years ago, he'd be in more pain."

The fabric's alive, squeezing Oscar's arms and legs until he falls like timber, the back of his head hitting the concrete. Unfortunately, he remains conscious, his blaming eyes narrowing in on me as he grunts.

If I were him, I'd cry out in agony. For Oscar, this is torture *du jour*. It's probably why he was so selfless in feeding information to Pete. I was wrong about him. No matter how much we loathe each other, his suffering makes me want to destroy the demon bitch ever more.

Real flames sprout and toss around Margery's upturned hairdo as she narrows a cigarette butt on me. "Get your ass in the warehouse. The only place you're going is to the Great Sand Dunes Park to bow to Azael."

My thoughts flash back to last night, when the hellhole quaked and erupted with the remains of sacrificed white warriors. Pete said the Earth's vibrations released a fallen angel by the name of Azael from his Blanca Peak tomb in the Sangre De Cristo Mountains. He insisted I'm his son.

"How do you know Azael's loose?" I ask.

"Who do you think helped him escape?" She smirks. "Honey, he's your father and my creator, making old Margery your big sister."

Nina gasps.

And my mouth gapes. I'm half shocked and half confused by her confession. Being the spawn of a fallen angel is hard enough to believe. Sharing my origin with a demon of her caliber is downright mind-blowing.

Margery snaps her fingers below my chin. "What, no smartass comeback? This is a first."

"Bullshit."

"If you've been talking to Pete, there's no way that asshole hasn't spilled the beans about your father, although he's unaware of my kinship. That's been a well-kept secret."

"We are not siblings." With a clenched jaw, I stare down at her.

"Listen, dumbass, I'm a demon, and you're Nephilim. My mother's a volcano. Your mother's a human. Regardless, we share the same maker. Our allegiance belongs to Azael." Margery draws on her cigarette and releases the smoke through her nose. "You can't deny our connection. Four days ago you begged me for a job. Yesterday we plugged up the hellhole to release Azael. Today you exposed this traitor." She twists the cherry on cigarette's smoldering butt into Oscar's forehead, putting it out and causing him to convulse.

"Sto, stop," I stutter, wishing there was something I could do. The sympathetic expression on Nina's face says she's feeling the same.

"Oh, Honey, I haven't even gotten started."

"Why did you have me sign a contract to work for Satan?" I ask, more to distract her from Oscar.

"Insurance," Margery says. "Everything I did, from courier contract to ensuring your warrant for damnation, was to guarantee you won't stray from Azael. You can't run to the CEO of Hell because Satan thinks *you* stopped the Gates of Hell from opening. And you can't run to God because He thinks *you* sacrificed part of Heaven's army. Now you're only safe with Old Margery."

"Safe…with you? *Ha!*" And she's reminding me how ridiculous it is that Satan insists he's the CEO of Hell, modernizing the underworld into a profitable corporation.

"God especially loathes your kind," Margery says. "Somehow, you're the only Nephilim who hasn't been hunted down and destroyed since the time of Noah, although I've yet to figure out why. Bottom line, you're stuck with me if you want to live.

A lightbulb goes off, realizing she ostensibly worked for Hell, but she's been faithful to an entombed fallen angel all along. A being who expects my loyalty after a sperm donation.

"Seemed impossible a dud like you could have escaped the hellhole last night." Margery mouths a fresh cigarette. "Let me guess. Oscar led you to Pete."

Not wanting to make things worse for him, I keep quiet and don't confirm she's guessed right again.

"Don't be naïve about Pete, Honey." Margery's eyes pulsate and spiral, so I look away or risk becoming hypnotized. "Has he admitted to re-imprisoning Azael on the day you were born? He deprived you of your father and rightful upbringing. If it weren't for Pete, you'd be at Azael's side, ruling over humankind. Instead, you grew up a loser."

While standing over her with arms crossed, I think how this is nuts. Everyone expects me to blindly be a part of *their* grand scheme. Again, it seems as if Nina and I are better off on our own.

"I get it." Phlegm gurgles in her throat as she says, "You're pissed about being set up. Get over it. Had to be done. Now take Blondie into the warehouse unless you prefer to watch the skaks finish off the traitor."

The hooded men hover over Oscar's motionless body. They uncover their heads and stare at each other, appearing unsure of Margery's intent. With shriveled skin and sunken cheeks, they belong in an Egyptian mummy exhibit. More horrifying, their receding lips bare cone-shaped teeth resembling those of a tiger fish.

"What are they?" I swallow hard.

"I told you. Skaks. Couriers I've been incubating in the sand dunes for the last half century. They're what happens when Old Margery and a hellhound spit in their graves. Unfortunately, they emerge as idiots." She approaches the skaks, her long bulbous fingers pushing them toward Oscar. "What are you waiting for? Use those teeth."

"Margery… they can't eat him." I rub the back of my neck and search for a way to stop the looming predators.

"It's their purpose, Honey. They'll feast their way through every human who denies your father's rule."

In an instant, a skak dives at Oscar's throat, ripping through his neck. His decapitated head rolls to the side, mouth gaping and tongue protruding.

With wide eyes, Nina screeches. Afraid she might bolt, I wave her over, but she replies by mouthing, "No."

On hands and knees, the monsters feast. Blood splatters across the patio. Intestines twist and twirl before being sucked in like spaghetti noodles.

My mind floods with regret. If I had stayed at the boarding house. If I had never met Margery. If a fallen angel hadn't claimed me as his son. Oscar would be alive.

Something inside me snaps. I rush the demon bitch, enveloping her hands. My grip locks around her fists with insane determination to rip off her hands so she can never throw another cursed cigarette. But electrical surges shoot along my forearms, and my palms burn as if I'm holding hot irons.

"Get him off me! Get him off me!" Margery's eyes turn black.

When no one comes to her aid, her fingers enlarge and nails morph into talons. I'm launched backward and bust my tailbone against a soda machine. The demon dispenser is knocked off balance, teetering to the ground with a loud crash. The machine's lights flicker despite it being unplugged.

Quickly, I roll away. This is the worst possible time for an evil essence to slither through the dispenser and take up residence along my spine.

"Bear!" Nina screams my nickname, a sign she's in control of her demon. She races over and yank my arm to help me up.

"We're getting out of here," I say. "I have a safe place for us to go."
This time, she agrees.

I spit on scorched palms. The pain's excruciating, but less distracting than Margery staring at her swollen talons with a stunned expression. Her flaming hair fizzles to sparks, and when she flicks her hand, only a puff of smoke releases.

Resembling a toddler in full tantrum, she jumps up and down. "Where…are…my…cigs?" Her wrinkles stretch and transform into black scales until she's a reptilian monster, stomping toward us, barking, "Get them."

With little to nothing left of Oscar but bones, the skaks are quick to attention, setting their sights on us being their dessert course. I grab Nina around the waist, throw her over my shoulder, and take off like *The Flash*.

Chapter 4

THIS TIME my sprint sputters to a stop as if I'm running out of gas. And Nina's missing from my arms.

What the hell?

I scan the surrounding dry grass and rocky terrain before spotting her twenty yards in the distance, at the side of the dirt road.

"Nina!"

Upon approach, one of the legs on her coveralls is shredded. She's immobile and unresponsive; a bloody streak reveals the extent of her wound.

Not only did I drop her, I dragged her. I hurt her bad.

Please be okay, please be okay.

My hands tremble as I yank my t-shirt over my head and wrap it around her leg where the flesh has been scraped to the bone, from hip to knee. But it's a worthless bandage.

What now?

While stroking her arm, I search for ways to help her without jeopardizing other body parts.

Pete.

I fumble in my pocket for the flip phone, then find the last number in the call history. After one ring, he answers. "Almost there. I know where you are."

"How?"

"GPS tracker on the cell." He blows out a loud sigh. "I would never leave you high and dry with Margery."

Reflecting on the trouble I've caused over the past twenty-four hours, how could I blame him if he did?

To the east, Pete's Hummer comes into view amid a cloud of dust. But within seconds, squawking off to the west drowns out the racing motor. A familiar flock of crows, the size of eagles, approaches. A few days ago, they protected me from God's army. I doubt it's their intent today.

Uncertain who will reach us first, I scoop up Nina's limp body, careful not to slip on the pool of blood. I hurry toward the Hummer, hoping I don't shift into hyper-speed and drag her again.

A few yards short of the vehicle, the black birds win the race, swooping in, wings whipping across my shoulders. Claws tear. Beaks peck. I swear they're gulping chunks of my flesh, possibly their way of taking me to Hell in pieces. All I can do is bear the pain and keep the pace.

Pete plows through the murder of crows and brakes to meet us. Through the cracked window, he yells, "Hurry! Put the girl inside!"

No shit!

I struggle to open the back door and place Nina onto the seat, but a wing knocks me off my feet and sends my glasses flying onto her stomach.

"Get in!" Pete says.

"I'm trying!" My arms flail, fighting off birds, but there are just too many. I'm about to take shelter beneath the vehicle when my hands glow and sting. Sparks shoot from my palms, and a bird bursts into a puff of smoke.

"Whoa."

Feathers fly everywhere and stick to the blood coating my chest. The others squawk, ascend, and hover.

I chuckle at the sight of a bent cigarette wedged in my palm.

Found your cigs, Margery.

I throw it at a crow in a nosedive, taking advantage of my pause. The bird freezes mid-flight, his eyes bulging from their sockets before he explodes like his brother.

Wow.

While pointing my palms skyward to hold them at bay, I climb into the back seat.

"Hang on." Pete flips a U-turn.

The crows follow and strike, one after another, rocking the vehicle.

"What," I say, "no protection spell on the Hummer?"

"Yes, but I suspect your active contract with Satan and your warrant for damnation are more powerful." His head bobs as he struggles to see past the flock swarming the windshield. "Cross your fingers they don't lift us off the ground."

"Open the sunroof." I lean between the front seats.

"Are you nuts? The crows will do anything to collect your bounty." He points at a white feather hanging from the rearview mirror. "A few strokes of that and Trisha will fly in with her white warriors."

"Trisha's warriors are dead… sacrificed—"

"Not all of them."

"Good to know, but I can get rid of the crows faster," I say because she's the only one I fear more than God and the CEO of Hell.

"You sure?"

"Yes. Trust me."

"Okay," Pete says, sounding unconvinced when he pushes a button on the dash.

The sunroof slides open, and I stick my hands through the slot, quick to aim my glowing palms skyward. As I twist through the window, each cigarette discharges with a sting that intensifies. After slaying a quarter of the flock, the remaining birds circle west and out of sight.

I collapse against the seat, feeling tarred and feathered.

"How did you repel the crows?" Pete asks. "What were those sparks?"

"Cigarettes," I say while unwrapping my shirt to check Nina's wound. She's healing but slowly. "Somehow, I absorbed Margery's cursed cigarettes."

"You what?"

"I'll show you later." With Nina resting on my lap, I wrap a nearby blanket around her motionless body and place my glasses over the bridge of my nose. "Nina's unresponsive. Will she be alright?"

"She's a courier. As long as her head is attached, she's alive." He peers over his shoulder. "Is she breathing?"

I lower my face to her nose but feel no breath on my cheek. Nor is her chest rising and falling. "No."

"Give her mouth-to-mouth," he says. "If she goes too long without oxygen, she'll go insane, and there's no curing crazy in a courier except through beheading."

Nina's gone through enough. If she loses her mind too…

While replacing her breath, I think how this is an unfortunate way for our lips to meet again.

"Candy," Pete says into his phone. "We're ten minutes out. Nina's with us and she's hurt. Tell Ulla and Inez to prepare for skin regeneration, and worst case, a decapitation."

Chapter 5

Back at the boarding house, under the early morning light, we might as well be in the middle of Nowhere, Colorado. The building is surrounded by nothing but dry sagebrush, drainage ravines, a dirt road, and one lonely tree. A golden glow on the distant foothills is the only beauty across the landscape.

The Hummer skids over the gravel driveway. Pete wails on the horn and parks. I'm quick to jump out, then carefully lift Nina into my arms. Returning here feels as if I've taken ten steps backward. Part of me wishes we were miles away from the mess I've made of our lives.

"Follow me to the apothecary." Pete rushes up the porch stairs, opens the front door, and leads me down a hallway paneled in dark-stained wood. When we enter the brightly lit kitchen, I smell pancakes and maple syrup, the same as earlier, before turning into a small side room.

The walls are covered in shelves that contain an assortment of old books and cookie jars in the shape of bears, racoons, and miscellaneous other wild animals. In the center sits a steel table more appropriate for a veterinarian's office.

"Put her down," Pete says.

I lay her on the cold metal surface, then stifle a sneeze brought on by dried herbs and other perfumed particles in the air.

"Ulla! Inez!" Pete calls toward the door, then he leans in close to Nina's face. "Good job. She's breathing again."

I nod and pray there's no permanent damage. To me, she still looks lifeless until I take her hand and she squeezes back. If she loses her mind, or worse, her head, I'll never forgive myself.

When a pudgy woman with two heads waddles into the room wearing a baby blue dress, I do a double take. The head with a braided salt-and-pepper bun, dark complexion, and sour expression has obviously belonged to the body since birth.

The head on the right has long, curly blond hair and appears to be an unnatural attachment. Even in her sixties, she's beautiful. Her rosy cheeks plump up from a sympathetic smile. "Oh, dear, what have we here?"

"Severe road rash," Pete says. "She also stopped breathing for a short time."

The two-headed lady peels the t-shirt bandage from Nina's leg, removing some of the regenerated muscle. I cringe at the sight of a third of her thigh still missing.

Pete pulls me aside, near the foot of the table.

The lady with the bun turns to me, and with a deep frown and Spanish accent she says, "You should have been here, breaking your contract with Hell. Instead, you sneak out. You do this."

"It was an accident." I cross my arms over my bare chest.

"No, you think with your wiener." She points at my crotch and asks Pete, "You want I make it disappear until he ends Azael?"

"Hey." I cover my zipper area and whisper to Pete, "Shouldn't she be focused on Nina?" My only hope is to avoid any more discussion about my favorite body part.

"Shh…" He swoops a hand toward the bitter woman. "Inez knows more about demons and immortals than anyone alive. Your friend couldn't be in better hands."

"Too much talk." Inez lifts Nina's eyelid. "She has purple iris. Is she still possessed?"

"Yes. Its name is Gita."

The two heads turn inward and stare at each other.

Pete takes a few steps backward. "Did you say Gita?"

"Yes." My temper flares.

Inez narrows in on me, her expression tight. "Of all the evil ones to bring here."

"You know Nina's demon?" I ask Pete.

"Gita occupied a courier I tried to save five years ago. During the exorcism, her essence went berserk and cut off his head," he says. "Her type of demon is dangerous but more so smart. Try to understand why we're unnerved by her return."

"I do, but Nina needs help. Please."

"Barry's correct," Ulla says while wiping away dirt and gravel around the wound. "We must mend her, regardless. Rescuing couriers is what we do here. Besides, we have put up with Pete's demon for many years. Cross your fingers Gita appreciates our act of kindness."

"Always the optimist." Inez grumbles and reaches inside an otter cookie jar. She sprinkles a black sparkly sand over Nina's wound as if she's seasoning soup.

Pete tilts his head with a twitch. "Wait. Why would Margery possess Nina with Gita?"

"Margery put a demon in her to control *me*, but she sent Oscar and me to retrieve it," I say. "I don't get why you trust him. He said he selected a rebellious essence to assist with our escape, but Gita's also goofy and reckless. And she seemed to want to stay at the warehouse. There's gotta be something you can do to stifle the demon's power over Nina."

They snap their attention to each other.

"What?" I ask.

No one responds, making me wonder what they're hiding.

After a long pause, Pete says, "Oscar would not sabotage you. Consider that after your hellhound attack, he saved your life and led you to me."

"I know, but…" I bite my lip. After watching Oscar die, arguing about his true agenda seems wrong.

Pete pulls out his cell. "Let me call him and clear this up."

"He won't answer." I hunch over.

"That's right, you have his phone. Hand it over."

"No. It's because he's dead." I retract and prepare for him to flip out. "Beheaded by a mummy courier, or skak as Margery calls them."

Ulla gasps.

"How?" Pete's face stiffens and so do his fists. "And what the hell is a skak?"

"I'm so sorry. I accidentally exposed Oscar to Margery as your mole." I step to the side to avoid any retaliation, but he manages to stay calm.

"Tell me more." He puts his fingers in the front pockets of his jeans and sucks air.

I divulge everything that occurred at the warehouse along with Margery's kinship to Azael. I end with Margery creating an army of mummified couriers under the sand dunes, and that the escaped fallen angel is hiding out there too.

Pete turns to the two-headed lady. "How did Margery keep this a secret? How could she build up such forces without us knowing?"

"We will investigate," Inez says, "but she possibly used volcanic magic. It is a thing Azael is known to control, but there is little information on the topic. Father Timothy will need to check the Vatican archives."

"Margery mentioned her mother is a volcano," I say. "Seemed crazy."

When Pete's shoulders twitch, Ulla asks him, "Is Boss okay?"

"Boss?" I ask.

He holds up his hand. "Not now."

"You agreed to full disclosure."

"I'll explain… I promise… soon."

"Make sure you keep up with the demon suppressant," Ulla says, piquing my curiosity. Last night, Pete said his demon was dormant. Has all this chaos revived it?

"Hey, can you give Nina some of that suppressant?"

But my request is ignored. Instead, the two-headed woman waddles to a nearby drawer, pulls out a folded space blanket, and shakes it loose. The cover crinkles as it's spreads over Nina up to her neck and tucked under her body.

"We should leave her alone to heal," Ulla says. "Besides, my sister and I have much to study."

"Should we strap her to the table?" Pete asks.

"What?" My heart skips a beat.

"Shish," Inez says. "The demon knows where she is and has yet to rattle the jars or flicker the lights to show displeasure. Let her focus on healing. Keep Barry in the house and all should be fine."

I kiss Nina's cheek. "Gita, it's me. We can go shoe shopping after you help Nina heal, but only if you behave."

Nina grins. Yesterday, Gita discovered a love of women's shoes, so hopefully she will comply.

"Appears Gita accepted the olive branch," Inez says, "but if she becomes destructive, Barry will clean up the mess."

Great. "Wouldn't she be calmer if you give her some of that suppressant?"

"No. That would upset Gita." Inez pokes my bare stomach. "So much blood. You shower now."

"Can I wait here instead?"

"No, no. Upstairs with you. We've laid out a change of clothes." Ulla turns to Pete. "And you must call your wife. She is very worried."

"Sure thing," he says.

Pete's married.

He hadn't mentioned it, but we've known each other less than twenty-four hours.

The two-headed lady toddles from the apothecary, the hem of her dress swaying against thick knees.

"Meet me in the dining room after you wash off the blood and feathers," Pete says. "It's time to eat the pancakes and break your contract with Satan."

"What is with the pancakes?" I ask.

"The antidote to Satan's contract is in them."

"Yeah, but pancakes suck."

"Do you really want to negotiate the menu with Inez?" Pete ushers me out of the kitchen.

Chapter 6

I ENTER THE dining room, showered and smelling like homemade citrus soap. A ray of sunlight shines through the sheer curtains that hang over a large picture window. Straight ahead, an antique clock reads five after seven. Two hours into the day, and I'm wondering if I'll live until lunchtime.

My mind continues to wander as I rest against a wall that's papered in pink roses on a beige background. Will breaking my contract with Satan hurt? Why do they think I'm the son of a fallen angel? Who am I, really?

A pear-shaped woman with short dirty-blond hair sits at the head of the mahogany table. A flowered spaghetti strap shirt covers her petite upper body. Below the belt, she's wearing hot-pink jeans, and her butt is so large that it hangs over the sides of the cushion. The remaining nine upholstered chairs are empty and in their places. I nod but might as well be invisible while she crams a handful of Swedish Fish candy into her mouth. She chews with puffy cheeks and guards the bowl of cherry treats with thin fingers. Apparently, she's unwilling to share her sugar high.

Her gaze is fixed on the television in the opposite corner. Pete enters, snatches the remote, and turns off a show that features women screaming at each other.

"Kissamyass." She lifts her wide bottom and reaches to take the control. When she misses, her fist pounds the table, jarring the treat bowl.

"Time to face reality." Pete settles into the chair on her left.

"It's reality TV," she says with attitude.

"Everything is about to become much more dramatic than your real housewives."

She turns to me and wrinkles her nose. "So, this is him."

"The name's Barry."

"More like Barry the Troublemaker. Barry the Selfish. Barry the Murderer."

After what happened to Oscar, it's a fair enough accusation, but I frown at her anyway. "Why are you here?"

"Meet Candy, your bodyguard," Pete says.

"More like your babysitter, and I won't put up with any of your shit."

"What exactly qualifies her to… babysitter me?"

"She used to work for Margery, at the Denver warehouse," he says, "which means her contract included superhuman strength. And she has a way of knowing when something is going to go wrong. Premonitions of sort."

"She got all that from Margery?" I ask, facing Pete.

"Hey." She taps her chest. "I can speak for myself, dork."

I repeat the question to Candy with a snotty attitude.

"No," she says, mimicking my tone. "The instincts are from my demon. If you haven't noticed, I'm a little bottom heavy."

"Oh, yeah… I noticed."

"Pervert," she mumbles.

"Let me explain," Pete interrupts, followed by a groan.

"Fine." She shoves another handful of Swedish Fish into her mouth.

"We tried to exorcise Candy's demon with a new process ten years ago and—"

"It went bad," she slurs with a mouthful of red confections.

"The demon essence melted into her butt," Pete says. "It can't speak directly to her anymore, but it lets her know when a situation doesn't feel right."

"Yeah," Candy says, "and the feeling I get about you is way off."

Before I can object, the lady with two heads carries in a short stack of pancakes topped with a ridiculously high dollop of whipped cream. She sets the silverware and plate on a placemat to the right of Candy, along with a pitcher of maple syrup.

"You sit," Inez says. "Swallow every bite."

After my morning, there's no fight left in me. I comply but have to ask, "Got any fruity cereal or edible gummy bears to sprinkle on top? And a bottle of gin would help me keep it down."

"No special orders." Inez twists my ear. "You stay sober."

"Ow, ow, ow." I cower away from her grip. Feels like I'm a kid again, forced to eat all my broccoli.

While the two-headed lady shuffles out of the room, I ask, "How's Nina?"

"Mind your business," Inez says. "Eat."

Not wanting another ear twist, I give up, slip the knife between layers, and lift the top one. My insides squirm at what I'm about to put in my mouth. "Bleck."

"Shouldn't have peeked." Candy snickers.

There's a good reason for the blanket of whipped cream. It hides insects. They made the stack from a batter heavy on thorax, legs, and wings. Limbs appear to wiggle, and I'm afraid to ask what the tiny white beads might be. I sit back and make a wish to wake up from this nightmare.

"How do you expect me to eat this?"

"With plenty of syrup." Pete clears his throat. "Consume every last bite if you want the antidote to work the first time."

First time?

Following his advice, I pour all the maple syrup around the edge of the pancakes, then hold up the pitcher and ask, "Any chance I can get more?"

Candy leans in. "Some cultures consider bugs a delicacy." Red goo from the Swedish Fish coats her teeth and lips. I'm starting to realize Candy is more of a nickname.

"Be thankful Inez has perfected the formula," he says, "and Ulla has done a fine job of masking the flavor from the original version."

"And be grateful it no longer has a hint of fermented trash dump." Candy grins, appearing to delight in my pain.

My hands heat up, ready to retaliate. But they also tremble as the fork cuts through the short stack with a snap, crackle, crunch, like squashing a beetle in a paper towel. While taking in a mouthful, I inhale the stench of worms and rotting leaves. So much for Ulla perfecting the recipe. But if this does disconnect me from Satan, it'll all be worth it.

"Careful, the white beads are salamander eyeballs." Candy smirks. "They pop when you bite them."

"Alright, enough with the teasing." Pete redirects his attention to me. "Father Timothy will arrive in a few hours. He can best explain the seriousness of the situation with Azael."

This should be interesting. We spent a lot of time together during my school years. Father Timothy was my counselor, and I was a constant pain in his ass. Back then, he was the only one who stood up for me, and he encouraged me to learn as much as I could about computers and technology. Now I find out he knew my lineage and was spying on me for years. Where was he when Margery trapped me into her contract from Hell?

After swallowing a mouthful of needle-sized legs that scrape my throat, I adjust my glasses and fight my gag reflex so I can ask, "What does my priest have to do with any of this?"

"During Azael's previous escape, Father Timothy and I apprehended him on the same day you were born." Pete shudders and closes his eyes. "Correction. My demon threw the Sword of Sin that captured Azael."

"A sword captured Azael?" I ask.

"It weakens angels when it's near them. Stab a fallen angel with it and they implode into a walnut-sized sphere, which makes it easier to imprison them in their tomb."

How could your demon throw a weapon?" I ask.

"Let's wait for Father Timothy." Pete twitches.

"Boss freaking out?" Candy asks.

"He just wants the credit," Pete says, "and he's due. If I let him, he'd waste the morning, telling the story."

"This Boss, he possesses you? I thought you said he's dormant." I shove a huge forkful of pancakes into my mouth and gulp it down.

"Yes," he says, "Boss was dormant, but he had a few choice words to say when Margery called to brag that you had signed your life over to Satan. Then we found out about Azael's escape. At first, he seemed on board to help eliminate your father, but now he's in panic mode."

"Which is the reason for the demon suppressant?"

"Boss has no influence over me. Ulla and Inez stopped that ability a long time ago, but his voice is still in my head. The suppressant calms him a bit. Unfortunately, it doesn't stifle his opinions."

"He's just worried about the curse Inez put on him," Candy says. "His demon essence can't be unfused from Pete's spine. If Pete loses his head, Boss will be stuck in his grave. He would have to go for an eternity without porn."

"Hey, that's more information than anyone needs to know." Pete says.

"Why can't any of this be done to Gita?"

"Barry, please, let Nina heal first. We'll figure something out later." Pete shifts the conversation. "There are higher priorities right now, like you understanding how dangerous your father is to humankind… and figuring out how you'll end him."

"Except Margery's sure Azael's destined to rule Earth with me by his side. Either job sounds ridiculous." I rub my forehead where an ache is starting. "If Boss captured my father once before, he has a better chance of success than I do. You guys should go after him again and leave me out of it."

Their awkward silence says I won't be skipping out on their agenda.

"All the rest of us can do is re-imprison Azael until he escapes again." Pete gnaws at his thumbnail. "You, well, your mother is a Daughter of Light, made by God to create a special child with a fallen angel. Being the first of your kind, you can wipe Azael's existence, permanently."

Another roller coaster of resentment against Father Timothy stirs in my stomach. Or maybe it's Ulla and Inez's pancakes. I wave the fork and say, "Why should I work with a priest who lied to me my entire life? Or anyone… or any being, who insists I fulfill some grand scheme?"

"Sorry. You're upset. Maybe I've said too much." Pete runs his fingers through his pompadour, but not a hair is mussed out of place. "We should wait for Father Timothy to speak for himself."

"Fine." I pause, needing a break from the pancakes but more so a hiatus from what's become of my life.

Candy keeps the conversation rolling when she asks, "What is up with Margery working with Azael? How long has that been going on?"

"She's the master of deception," Pete says. "Twenty-two years ago, we thought Azael's escape was an accidental result of the hellhole closing. Considering his most recent release mimics his last, it's now obvious that Margery devised both."

The fact that it took them this long to figure it out has me coughing pancake spit. Bug particles fly through the air and land in Candy's bowl of Swedish Fish. Time stops until she forces air out of her nose. Either she's going to cry or put a fork in my forehead.

I hold up a hand. "Sorry. It was an accident. I'll keep my head down. Look." I gobble every remaining bite as if I'm in an eating competition.

She pushes her bowl aside and settles back in her seat. "You absolutely do need a babysitter."

As a wave of cramps kicks in, I regretfully clutch my gut. "How bad is this going to hurt?"

"It won't be pretty for a few hours," Pete says. "Please, no running off. Let your body absorb the antidote."

I nod and consider how a run would induce vomiting, and I'd rather poke my eyes out than ingest another short stack.

Pete then asks me, "How do you move so fast? And what's the story with stealing Margery's cigarettes? It's got to be something you can use against Azael."

"Hyper-speed started after a trip to Hell's refugee camp. It's how I traveled while I was there. I somehow brought the ability back with me, although I have no clue how. Today, at the warehouse, I grabbed Margery's hands, and now I can shoot cigarettes from my palms. It's flakey how I do it, but I seem to absorb abilities from places and beings."

With wide eyes, Candy bounces in her seat. "Shoot… shoot a cigarette. Show us how—"

"Later," Pete says. "Barry needs to let the antidote sink in."

"Tell us about the refugee camp?" Candy says. "What's it like?"

"You don't want to know." At least she's interested and warming up. "The place is miserable, and I don't want to relive anything about being there."

"Good incentive to keep your head so you don't get sent there." She turns up an evil grin. "Should make my babysitting job easier, but I'm not counting on it."

"That better not be a threat," I say.

"Stay clear of Candy's sweets," Pete says, "and you'll be fine."

"Not funny," she says, but we all laugh anyway.

The flavor of worms accosts my taste buds as I stand. *Toothpaste*, I think. "Can I go upstairs and brush my teeth?"

"Yes." Pete stands and pulls a cell phone out of his pocket. He slides it across the table. "While you're up there, call your mother."

"Weren't those pancakes torture enough?" Instantly, guilt churns in my gut.

"She's worried." Pete frowns and his nostrils flare. "All she can do is sit by and hope you don't get your head bitten off by a hellhound again."

"Mom knows about that?"

"Unfortunately, yes," he says.

Smart thinking by Pete. A conversation with Mom is a guaranteed two-hour lecture that will keep me grounded long enough to break my contract with Satan.

"Lay down and let the antidote do its thing," Pete says. "I'll come get you when Father Timothy arrives."

Chapter 7

THE BED I stayed in last night is comfortable despite my continued cramping. Well, until it vibrates. According to the alarm clock on the nightstand, only twenty minutes of peacetime have elapsed since I left the dining room. And I still haven't built up the nerve to call my mom.

The house creaks and moans and groans.

My grip on the quilt tightens. *What now?*

This better not be a Margery induced earthquake. My heart races, realizing it's more likely Gita.

Shit!

I jump up and grab my glasses, then rush downstairs and pause near the entryway.

"Bitch, Kissamyass!" Candy adds a half dozen more insults where she stands in the kitchen doorway.

This can't be good.

"What's going on?" Shifting side to side, I struggle to see past Candy, blocking the scene with her freakishly large butt.

Pete squeezes beside her and approaches in a hurry. "Let's go." He hooks my arm and reaches for the doorknob.

"Why?" While part of me wants to further investigate the dispute, I comply and follow him onto the porch.

"Watch out!" He pulls me out of the way a half-second before Candy flies backward alongside us. With an oomph, she skids across the lawn.

This is bad… really bad.

Nina runs through the entrance, still wearing shredded and blood-soaked coveralls.

"What's wrong?" I yell at Nina's fleeing backside, but this has to be Gita doing.

She ignores me and jumps into the driver's seat of the Hummer. The door locks snap. The engine starts. The wheels scrape.

"Let her go." Pete tugs at my shirt.

This time I break away, calling out for Nina to wait while she backs into the street. Like an idiot, I wave my arms and chase the vehicle. Continued cramping and the threat of vomiting up bugs stifles my need for speed. That and a fear of smashing my skull into the Hummer's giant spare tire.

Standing in the middle of the road, my jaw clenched, I watch the taillights disappear into the distance… and curse Candy.

Nina's gone.

We're separated, again.

A loud crash ends my self-pity party. I spin around to find the boardinghouse is missing, collapsed into a sinkhole. Centered ten feet below ground-level, the chimney, half the roof shingles, and a few boards are all that's in sight.

Damn! My stomach drops. While Candy may have provoked Nina's departure, they'll blame me for the condition of the building.

Pete's frozen on the walkway, staring into the pit, the sun glaring off his black hair. Loose strands dance in the breeze.

I drag my feet across the gravel driveway and pause beside Pete. "Where's Candy and the woman with two heads?"

"They have names." Candy exits the detached garage, limping on one lime-green Croc and carrying a bundle of rope. Her butt's smeared with grass stains. "Ulla and Inez are in that pit because you brought Nina and Gita into our home."

There it is, just as expected. It's all my fault.

"How could a demon, contained in a human being, do so much

damage?" I ask.

"Such an idiot." Candy ties the rope around the only tree for a mile, throws the other end into the hole, and tugs to confirm it's secure.

"You're not going down there, are you?" I ask. "The house is unsafe, and Ulla and Inez are probably dead."

"Kissamyass," she says in a high-pitched whine that's punctuated with sniffles.

"Hey!" Pete throws up his hands and his body jerks. "We're on the same team. If we can't get along and work together, how can we fight Azael?"

"Save the pep talk." After flipping me the bird, she lowers herself into the crater.

"I'm sorry," I say. "You're right. I shouldn't have brought Nina here. I just felt responsible for everything that's happened to her." Realizing no one is buying my apology or excuse, I grasp the rope and ask, "Should we help?"

"Definitely not," Pete says. "In fact, she might be offended if you lend a hand."

"A little disturbing that you're encouraging her."

"A lot disturbing you would give up on Ulla and Inez," he says. "Besides, she can literally lift the Hummer over her head. You can't argue with that."

The roof creaks and snaps as she steps across shingles. Without hesitation, she punches open a hole large enough to slip through. I make a mental note to stay clear of her right hook.

We awkwardly stand by, the breeze intensifying and dark clouds forming over the foothills.

"Weather report predicting rain?" I say to break the silence.

"Nope. Supposed to be a sunny day." He scans the area. "Did you call your mother?

"Nope."

"Why not?"

I avoid the topic and build up the courage to ask, "What happened between Candy and Gita?"

"She went into the apothecary and an argument started, but I couldn't hear what they were saying. When I tried to separate them, I panicked and said we should have tied up Nina. After that, the house began to rattle."

The guilt in my gut dissipates while I glare at him. This time *he* should have known better. "Why didn't you come get me?"

"In hindsight…"

I want to hit him but Candy's surfacing. "Found 'em!" She and Ulla rise through the hole in the roof, but Inez appears stuck.

"Slow down, dammit!" Inez lets out a muffled scream, then her head pops out, her hair and face covered in white powder.

"Thank God," Pete says.

The two-headed lady piggybacks Candy as they emerge through the roof shingles. Like a broken record, Ulla sings, "Oops, I did it again."

"She loves Britney Spears, but she also sounds loopy," Pete says. "Let's hope she doesn't have a concussion."

We reach for the rope and help pull them to safety, but Pete's dead-on about Candy's amazing strength and concentration.

The woman with two heads collapses on the ground, Inez struggling to catch her breath. Ulla continues to sing an odd mix of Britney Spears songs while Candy hovers, picking wood slivers out of both the women's hair.

"Did Ulla hit her head?" Pete asks.

"We're fine." Inez slaps Candy's hand. "Back off."

"Are you sure?" He stares into Ulla's eyes.

"She's attached to my body. I think I would know." She turns to me with a scrunched scowl and waves an accusing finger. "You, however, are in for a world of hurt."

I take a few steps backward, in case she's packing something dark and magical in her housecoat. Instead of apologizing, I say, "I offered to stay with Nina to keep her calm. Now she's gone… God knows where."

"She doesn't need you," Candy says. "She doesn't want you. She's got the hots for your father."

"That's disgusting. What's your problem?" I frown and grit my teeth.

"Stop it." Pete twitches. "Both of you, stop it."

"He needs to know the truth, so he stops chasing after something he can't have." Candy crosses her arms and rocks them as if she's holding a baby. "Nina and Azael and a baby carriage."

I face Pete, my body stiff. "What is she talking about?"

After a long pause, he says, "Nina is a Daughter of Light, like your mother. She'll do anything to be with your father now that he's escaped his tomb."

With my hand over my mouth, I peer the direction Nina pulled away in the Hummer. This could explain her hesitation at the warehouse, but there has to be another explanation. "That's a lie!"

Pete sighs. "No… it's true."

Chapter 8

IDROP TO the ground and sit with my head between my knees, trying to make sense of Nina lusting after Azael.

She would never.

Or would she?

With my father?

Bullshit.

Pete stands over me and touches my shoulder. "You okay, Barry?"

"Why would God want to create more of my kind? He hates Nephilim."

"Isn't it obvious. It's in case you fail," he says while he starts to pace. "Sorry for not mentioning it. Father Timothy ordered me not to tell you about Nina, which is why you should discuss this with him."

I lift my head. "The cat's already out of the bag. You might as well spill your guts."

"It's not my place to explain some things." After a long pause, Pete adds, "We should go to the hotel in Trinidad, where the rest of my crew are staying."

"Rest of your crew?" I stand and brush dust off my pants.

"Yeah, they're working on a land leasing project to keep evil at a minimum in Southern Colorado. It helps fund my operation to save couriers. Let me call Father Timothy and have him meet us there."

Candy swipes at her phone. "Since Azael's girlfriend stole our vehicle, I'll request a ride share before you call him."

Unamused by her dig, I force a laugh, then turn away to watch dust stirring across the terrain and tumbleweeds bounding in the distance.

"Barry, let her go for now." Pete's voice rises over the whistling wind. "Your number one priority is understanding your purpose in eliminating Azael."

"All I'm saying is Nina's life can't play out like my mother's before I'm given a chance to succeed." Protecting her is the least these people can do, considering they've lied to me about everything.

Candy hands Pete the cell phone, then stomps closer to me with a single-shoe limp, a heavy breeze tussling her hair. "If you try to run again, I'll knock you down so fast."

Good luck catching me.

I focus on a solitary dark cloud, the width of a baseball diamond, floating our direction at a freakish speed.

"That cloud looks ominous." Candy approaches the two-headed lady and points. "Sent by Satan?"

"Devious," Inez yells above the wind, "but not from Hell."

When it swirls, and a cone forms at the center, I'm reminded of a recent storm. Gusts so strong, they hurled me down a ravine. "I agree with Inez."

"How would you know, smart guy?" Candy blinks and rubs her eyes. "Damn dust."

"A few days ago," I shout, "I barely escaped a tornado south of Denver while driving one of Margery's vans, but other couriers were sucked inside it. I thought God sent the twister."

They stare at me, appearing confused. Makes me question how these people can support me when they have no idea what Margery's been up to all the years I've been growing up.

After a deep breath, I say, "Remember what I told you about Margery transforming couriers into skaks? Those toothy mummies that ate Oscar? She confessed that she's been collecting the drivers. What if she's gathering them with tornados? This storm is possibly her doing."

"Or Azael's." Candy scurries in a circle. "Shit, we've got to hide. Everyone, into the hole!"

"Are you nuts?" I say. "Risking a hundred broken bones is safer than sinking underground in a town near the Hellmouth."

"We stay on land," Inez says. "We chant. We protect."

Locking arms, we huddle over the two-headed lady as they recite a spell that would tie my tongue. An invisible dome encases us, breaking the airstream. Dirt flows directly above, as do twigs and tumbleweeds.

While the whirling cloud continues to hover, the funnel takes aim, firing dark spherical objects the size of basketballs. Each shot ricochets off the protective sphere and lands on the ground a few feet away, surrounding our barrier.

I worry the cannonballs will explode until I recognize the ammunition as heads. *Human heads.*

Once Azael's message has been delivered, the cloud implodes with a deafening boom that pops my ears. The sky clears, and the wind dissipates along with our shield.

"Look at the veils." Pete pivots away from us, his murmurs appearing to be a private discussion with Boss. Then he tells us, "They're nuns, from Sisters of the Divine Heart Convent."

"Not all of them." Candy drops to her knees and weeps. "This one's Father Timothy."

"What?" I choke on a lump in my throat. This can't be happening.

Brain matter oozes from the back of the caved-in skull, but the hairline, blue eyes, and small nose are unmistakably his. Of course, Azael has killed the man who knows him best and helped to re-imprison him the year I was born. Did he also do it because the priest has been my only father figure?

Pete hands the cell phone to Candy. "Please change our ride share to the convent, so we can check on the other nuns. If Azael destroyed the building, we'll need to move the survivors to the hotel, if there are any."

With my fists at my sides, I turn toward the road. "I'm going to wipe the bastard's existence."

"Yes, you are," Pete says, "and we're going to help, but not yet. Right now, the nuns are our priority. Let's gather the heads and put them in the garage before our ride gets here."

But my mind's too focused on revenge. I want to charge like a bull.

Find him, I tell my feet. *Find Azael.*

Chapter 9

So far, running at hyper-speed has proven useful, but a blow to my chest interrupts this trip. I fly backward and land on my tailbone with my legs spread across the rocky ground. I shake my head and catch my breath.

What the hell?

Then the pain strikes, but it's overshadowed by nausea, which shifts my attention to keeping down the antidote. With my jaw clenched, I retch, then turn to the side and try to swallow. The regurgitation force is too great. Pancakes and insects and bugs spray from my nose. After a few gagging coughs, I spit.

Idiot! I'm an idiot. And I tried so hard to cancel my contract with Satan. Now I'm God knows where…

A blinding, golden light looms and dims into a winged figure. Have I run smack into Azael? Nope, worse. Trisha, the angel apprentice, stands with her arms crossed over a white silk blouse, and she's tapping a strappy white Stiletto, an indication she's about to go ballistic. She has every right to be angry. Because of me, her warriors were sacrificed to seal a hellhole, although not on purpose.

"What is wrong with you?" Trisha stomps a pointy toe near my family jewels.

My ass cheeks tighten, and I clutch my pants zipper. A cigarette pops out of my palm and electrifies my hands and crotch, bringing new meaning to becoming my own worst enemy.

Trisha laughs, then says in a high-pitched voice, "Don't even think about firing one of those things at me."

"If you're going to behead me, do it quickly." I throw the smoldering butt aside.

"I wish, but God thinks you're… special." Trisha's wings pull-in as she steps back, probably because I'm fixated on the dissipating glow under her white miniskirt. How could I not be tempted by her long shapely legs? With smooth caramel skin, dark eyes, and brown wavy hair, she looks similar to a young Jennifer Lopez. There's also her intoxicating rose-scented perfume. Not so nice mixed with reeking vomit.

"I don't get why God would want anything to do with me?"

"After watching over every stupid decision you've made today, it's a true mystery. Unfortunately, I've been assigned to knock some sense into you."

Creepy and somehow sexy that she's been keeping an eye on me. Wonder if she peeped while I showered.

"Stopping me like that," I say, "you're taking that order a little too seriously."

"Poor baby. Does it hurt?"

"Why should I listen to you?" I glare up at her.

"Because you owe me." Trisha waves a fist. "And I will pummel you if you don't."

"Okay. Fine." I do feel obligated for what I put her through. "Get in line with everyone else on my ass about assassinating Azael."

"Fair enough." She reaches to help me up. At the same time, a tickle hits my throat and rushes into my nasal cavity, forcing a sneeze. Salamander eyeballs and insect parts spurt from my nostrils and settle on her shoes.

I laugh and wipe my nose.

"Such a fuck up." She shakes her head and swirls a finger in the air. The chunks and sour odor disappear. "Won't be so funny when you're chowing down on another dose of the antidote."

"Thanks for the reminder."

"At your service." She bows.

I scan beyond a nearby drop off and into a desolate chasm that's a mix of sand, sparse trees, and boulders. The beating sun has my armpits turning wet and sticky. "Where are we?"

"Poison Canyon. West of those mountains is the Great Sand Dunes National Park, where Azael is hiding, and Nina is headed." Then she points to large rock formations. "My cave is down there." She closes in and pokes my shoulder with a long, red manicured fingernail. "Don't change the subject. Why are you chasing Nina, *again*, while innocent people are being killed? Not to mention you still haven't apologized for what you did to my warriors last night."

"I wasn't." I mutter and avoid eye contact, the burning in my gut now from guilt instead of Inez's pancakes.

"This isn't a video game with a reset button." She gets bouncy when she's mad, luring my gaze to her chest. "Are you listening to me?"

"Of course." I clear my throat and focus on her forehead. "I wasn't following Nina. I wanted Azael."

"What?"

"If you've been watching me, you know I can run extra fast."

"Uh huh." She twirls a lock of hair around a finger.

"The way it works, I consider a destination and my feet go there. Before taking off, I was furious. I wanted to destroy my father."

"Pursuing a fallen angel by yourself is… *insane*."

"Everything piled up with the house collapsing, being pelted with holy heads… finding out Nina's a Daughter of Light. How can you people expect her to do what my mother—"

"Poor Barry…" She rolls her eyes.

"Everyone expects me to destroy Azael, but no one believes I can do it. It's not fair Nina has to deliver the next me because I'm likely to fail. Hell, there's no chance of success when I'm being kept in the dark. How am I supposed to trust anyone?"

"Trust is a two-way street."

"That's my point."

"Father Timothy was supposed to explain—"

"Pete used the same excuse." My jaw clenches.

"Fine." She puts her hands on her hips. "No more lectures. You deserve answers."

"Now?"

"Yes. Now."

Chapter 10

"**A**ZAEL FELL with Satan,"Trisha says, "and the two are driven by pride and arrogance, but they have opposite agendas. While Hell feeds off the fallout of humankind's free will, your father intends to prove how wrong God was for granting free will. Azael believes people require saving. Given a chance, he'll reign over the Earth with his children, and humans will live by his design."

Of all she mentioned, being a part of a fallen angel's royal family resonates as fascinating, although more so creepy if it means standing beside Margery, who insists she's my sister. Sends a chill along my spine despite the hot, dry weather.

I slump. "And God made me to prevent this loss of autonomy?"

"Yes, but more so your job is to eliminate Azael from existence." She hesitates before adding, "It sounds impossible, especially considering this will be the first erasure of an angel, light or dark."

"Hilarious that God expects me to do his dirty work."

She steps closer "If it makes you feel better, you're not alone."

"Oh, yeah, so much better."

"I, too, had doubts, but in the last few days, you've acquired quite the abilities." She giggles. "How in the world did you manage to steal Margery's favorite pastime?"

"Weren't you watching?"

"She placed extra protection on the warehouse and the surrounding area. The place is completely dark to angels."

I tell her everything that happened at the warehouse, reveling in the fact that I can steal a demon's magic, but shift the conversation to my prime worry. "Cut the crap. We need to discuss Nina being a Daughter of Light?"

"Of all your priorities," Trisha says. "What is with her?"

"Lay off. Everything Nina's faced this week is my fault."

"Are you in love with her?"

"This is about preventing her suffering before I have a chance to eliminate my father."

Trisha takes a deep breath. "Look, every time Azael breaks out, he seeks holy women to impregnate—in recent centuries, nuns. The resulting children strengthen him. But he was always hunted down and re-imprisoned. And his newly born offspring were killed. You are the first Nephilim that God has allowed to exist because your mother is a Daughter of Light."

"And your point is?"

"You exist to destroy your father, although we're just learning how that might be possible. Having more of your kind around during this escape could further incapacitate him, especially if you fail."

There it is over again. No one believes in me. I want to argue she's wrong, but a question comes to mind. "Azael has a fetish for holy women, but Nina's not—"

"No," Trisha says, "although she should be. It's equally disturbing you've both signed contracts with Satan, and she's currently possessed by a demon. Neither of your lives developed as expected."

"God's The All Mighty, The All Powerful. Why didn't He intervene? Ensure His desired paths for us?"

"If the ways of people were as easy as having God intervene, we'd be living in utopia, bliss, paradise," she says. "Instead, humans live under constant uncertainty. Free will has interfered with God's intentions for you both. And as I mentioned earlier, that's the very thing you are here to preserve."

"Kind of ironic, but is this course we're on a good thing or a bad thing?"

"Only time will tell, but now that Azael's loose, it's important to remove all distractions from your life, including Nina. It's why Pete wanted you to trust that Oscar would keep her safe."

"Why isn't anyone worried a fallen angel and possessed Daughter of Light could be a more dangerous combination?"

"Some fallen angles are skilled at evading God, but Daughters of Light have proven to be a valuable distraction for Azael. Pete and Father Timothy caught him last escape due to a bit of luck and your mother's wiles. Nina could do the same."

"You better hope so," I say, making note that she's avoiding my question. "Margery's being extra cautious about building an army before Azael produces more siblings."

"Until Nina's introduced to Azael, it's unclear what will happen."

"Is Margery aware of the Daughters of Light?"

"She shouldn't be, but there's never any telling with her."

"Sounds like there are more risks than anyone will admit." I glare at her, widen my stance, and add, "Does anyone care Nina could be the next casualty?"

Her expression straightens as she moves in closer. "Are you sensing any urges to defect to your father's side?"

I frown and wonder why she shifted the conversation, yet again. Does this mean they don't care if Nina dies? How many other Daughters of Light do they have in the queue, ready to replace me?

"Where the hell is that coming from?" I ask. "The thought of being anywhere near Margery is deterrent enough."

"All I'm saying, if you detect a draw to him, tell someone ASAP."

I nod and step closer.

"Barry, seriously, you're not alone, but we can't force you to follow orders. You have free will, and you've already gotten into plenty of trouble. Know that you're being watched, very closely. Turn against God…" Her finger slices across her neck as she levitates to my level, bringing us nose to nose.

In the middle of a staring contest, I say, "I'm fine. Sympathizing with Nina doesn't mean I'll turn against the world. Any Daughter of Light deserves protection against Azael until I fail."

Trisha purses her lips and places her hands on my shoulders. "Can you accept that she'll want no one but Azael? That she'll never love you?"

Am I crazy? Is Trisha jealous?

While gazing into her brilliant eyes, I'm drawn in.

I can't help myself. I kiss her.

Blinding light and warmth engulf us. My body releases as if I'm on a million doses of Ecstasy, floating higher and higher, reaching to draw her in. Suspended midair, my tongue gropes like an addict, desperate for another fix.

But Trisha's not there.

"Hey, goofy." She giggles, bringing me back to reality. "I'm confused. You love Nina but kiss me. You are Azael's son."

"Put me down." My legs flail as I mutter, "Crazy bitch."

"What were you hoping to accomplish?" she asks with a crooked smile.

"Okay, stupid move. Lesson learned."

"But an interesting move at that." Trisha's face continues to glow as she strokes her lower lip.

"Interesting? Pshaw." Sure, I'm far from a Don Juan, but she sounds as if our kiss was a TED Talk.

"Kissing is a human expression, Barry. You're Nephilim, only sharing half my lineage. I was shocked to feel a spark when our lips met," she says. "I suppose I liked it but suspending your ass while you mouthed the air was so much more satisfying."

With a palm up, I take aim and shoot a cigarette at her.

She waves a finger and shakes her head again. The butt falls short. "*Do not* throw those things at me."

"Then put me down."

"You're not going anywhere until you agree to stay focused on eliminating Azael."

"I am focused," I say. "All I'm asking, keep Nina away from my father. I'll do anything you want, and if I fail, you can hand her over to him."

"Wow. After that kiss, you're still thinking about *her*?"

"You *are* jealous?"

She flips me and drops me on my head.

"*Ahh…!*" I roll onto my side, collect my glasses, and jump to my feet. "That wasn't necessary."

"You asked for it." She inspects her fingernails as though bored.

"Are you sure you work for God? Because you're pretty damn sadistic!"

"Let me remind you how many years I've been chasing couriers. Why should I be nice?" A sparkle flickers in one of her eyes. "Anyway, you won't give up on Nina, so I agree to your terms. I'll personally protect her, and *when* you fail, I'll drop her in Azael's lap."

"Agreed," I'm quick to say.

"While there's more to discuss," she says, "the rest can wait until after I round up Nina. So, take those speedy feet to the Super 8 Hotel off the highway in Trinidad. Pete has a crew there—"

"Yeah, he mentioned it."

"Until Ulla and Inez prepare another antidote, it's the safest place for you to be."

"Seriously. More pancakes?"

"Shouldn't have run away from the boarding house," she says with an evil grin. "Ask for Fig at the hotel. She'll get you settled and introduce you to the team. When Pete and I arrive, we'll talk more about the next steps."

"And Nina?"

"Cross your fingers I find her before Margery does."

Chapter 11

THIS TIME my feet bring me to the northern part of Trinidad, a popular Colorado stop-off for travelers between New Mexico and Denver. Gas stations, fast-food chains, and hotels surround the highway, as does the aroma of deep-fried foods and the sound of racing automobile engines.

The parking lot at the Super 8 Hotel appears deserted as I approach the covered entrance. An empty stomach and a nervous tic in my eye beg me to avoid Pete and detour to a pizza joint instead. After this morning, they may handcuff me and lock me in the hotel's basement.

While opening the front door, I decide to start with an apology and hope for the best.

A slim, thirty-something woman with brown hair, cut in a manly style, stands behind the check-in desk. She's wearing a wide smile and a maroon polo with the company logo.

"I'm looking for Fig." I push my glasses up the bridge of my nose and am amazed at the fact that they continue to stay on during a run.

"Found me. Are you Barry?" Her perky voice and glow are inviting. Maybe I'm not in too much hot water.

"Yep." I say.

"Pete's on his way with Candy and the nuns." She holds out a plastic key card. "He told me to assign you to a room and have you meet his crew chief, Nassar."

"Okay." I breathe a sigh of relief that Pete hasn't arrived yet, and that some of the nuns are still alive.

"Could you please take that with you?" She points to the end of the desk, at a blue crate packed with unopened liquor bottles.

I side shuffle to it and pull out a bottle with clear liquid. *Gin. Yes.*

When I turn back to say thanks, Fig has changed into a man. I lift an eyebrow.

In a much deeper voice and wearing the same bright expression, Fig says, "Could you also tell everyone pizza delivery is expected any minute."

"Sure thing." I grasp the handles on the crate. "What luck. I considered stopping for pizza before coming here."

"Thank you." As I turn toward Fig, he's become a she again and delivers a wink. "It's my job to keep the guests happy."

Changing sexes at will and psychic too? Nothing's shocking anymore.

Halfway to my room, two men and a woman approach. While the men blend in with their business casual dress and ordinary faces, the woman's hair is a mix of black and white spikes, comparable to an anime cartoon. We all freeze. My eyes are drawn to tribal tattoos covering her exposed arms, chest, and neck. Bet the skin under her black tank top, jeans, and thigh-high boots is similarly adorned.

"Let's go," she says to the others, then yanks open a door marked with a green glowing exit sign.

I leave them behind, scanning room numbers along the musty hallway lined with stained red carpet. A sudden whiff of stale cigarettes has me spinning in a circle, sure Margery is nearby. Then I remember her hexed butts are in the palms of my hands. Besides, after Trisha's long lecture, why would she deliver me to the enemy? My mind immediately switches to Nina, and that she'd better be with Trisha by now.

The smell is more likely from the ex-couriers who live here, their breed indulging in the worst vices. It'd be perfect if one of them had a joint to calm my nerves before Pete arrives, but I'm not smelling the remnants of weed.

A Viking ax flies through an open door to my left and lands at my feet. I shiver, and the bottles clink in the crate. Too bad a hyper-speed exit is no longer an option. Instead, I step backward, put the liquor on the floor, and prepare for the next lethal weapon to launch my way.

A tall, burly guy wearing a navy-blue t-shirt and khaki cargo shorts rushes into the hallway. His rusty hair and full beard look as if they've been cut and styled with the ax. He smiles and extends a muscular, veiny arm to invite a handshake with chunky fingers. "Howdy, Chump."

What the hell?

Who's he calling a chump? He's the idiot who could have decapitated me.

A bald black man in a red embroidered silk robe struts on black patent-leather pumps out of an open doorway to my right. Below the short hem, athletic socks with two red stripes stretch to his knees. "Chump, are you harassing Barry?"

"That's your name?" I ask ax man. "Chump?"

"Yep." He puffs out well-defined pecs while we grasp hands.

The other guy takes his turn with an introduction. "Nassar. Crew chief."

"I guess you already know who I am." When we shake, I expect him to switch sexes like Fig, but he doesn't.

Nassar says to the other guy, "You need to spend more time sharpening the blades than throwing them around the hotel."

Ax man exhales hard, fluttering overgrown mustache hairs. "Weapons is my business, not yours."

"Have you finished preparing the lease packets?" the crew chief asks.

"Printer's broken," he says.

"It's always something with you."

"Fuck you." Chump pulls a bottle of bourbon from the crate, then picks up the ax, swings it over his shoulder, and stomps into his room. The pockets of his cargo shorts jingle as if he's carrying twenty dollars in loose change.

In hopes of calming the conflict, I say, "The pizza will be here soon."

"Good." Nassar sashays after Chump with a manicured hand on his waist. "Maybe a full stomach will stifle his excuses."

I follow, hauling the crate to a spot inside the doorway, then grab a bottle of gin for myself and scan the vast space with fascination. Chump's staying in a dayroom with a military-style bunk shoved straight ahead and under a window. Racks of fifty or more medieval axes, swords, daggers, and other assorted sharp objects line most of the walls. Given a pop quiz on their technical names and proper uses, I'd fail. There's an immaculate order he devotes to the weapons. I'm guessing he's a guy I want at my side in battle, but first I hope he'll teach me how to fight.

Two plastic banquet tables sit in the center of the room. The objects on top reveal his challenge with the broken printer and paperwork. Add in a disarray of manila envelopes and he appears to file by throwing things up in the air to find order in wherever they land.

Nassar pecks his head while saying, "How could one person make such a colossal mess?"

"Told you," he says, "weapons and dismembering demons is my specialty. Izi and her guys should do the leases."

I guzzle the gin to numb my nerves and wonder if he's referring to the people I saw near the lobby.

"I don't get it," Chump throws up his hands. "Why are we stuffing envelopes when we should be preparing for war with a fallen angel? The hellhole closed last night, and if Azael hands us our asses, who cares about the paperwork?"

"We won't lose." But I'm ignored, as if they are two more people who have zero confidence in me. Then again, I'm not sure I believe my own positive thinking.

"Still with avoiding your job." Nassar pops a hip. "How many times do we have to explain this to you? Besides this work paying for those weapons you prize, these leases prevent Satan's hellhole operation from expanding off of the Bellow's Ranch. They stop mining and oil exploration, the very thing that destabilized this region when the coal mines were active. If the Catholic Church didn't lease the mineral rights, developers might detonate a nuclear bomb of evil in southern Colorado."

Pete mentioned the leasing projects this morning, but this explanation has me tipping the bottle of gin again.

Nassar then says, "Yes, hunting down Barry's father is important, but if we don't get these leases signed, we'll be chasing down demons and damned souls that escape from Hell's refugee camp."

In walks a short guy, his face and torso covered by a tall stack of pizza boxes. His baggy jeans cover his shoes. "Help me out here," he says with a slight Spanish accent.

The tempting aroma of sausage, pepperoni, and parmesan cheese stifles the tension when Chump rushes to grab the boxes and spread them across the scattered paper.

"You'll grease up the leases," Nassar whines. "Are you trying to make more work for yourself?"

My stomach growls as I hurry to lift the lid on a box. Chump's hairy knuckles beat me to the largest slice of pepperoni. He snickers and, with the hand holding the bourbon, pounds his burly chest. Booze splashes onto his shirt. The sweet smell of cherry tickles my senses as I submit to taking a smaller piece.

Nassar hovers near the printer while we chow down. A few seconds later, he slams the paper drawer closed on his thumb. He squeals and hops around on one high heel, showing off amazing balance. "Damn you. There's nothing wrong with this machine. It needed more paper."

The new guy laughs open-mouthed, his chubby belly bouncing under an oversized yellow t-shirt. "What do you expect? In his day, they carved contracts in stone."

"Shut up, Javier." Chump pokes out his middle finger from the neck of the whiskey bottle he's holding.

"Should have had Izi's crew cover it," Javier says. "Speaking of… where are they?"

"None of your business," Nassar says.

Again, I wonder if they're arguing about the people I encountered in the hallway. Does seem odd that they left with such an important task unfinished.

"Did you let them leave the hotel?" Chump pounds his fist on the table, and the pizza boxes hop.

"They finished their leases and needed a break."

Chump spits food while he says, "If they took off, I'm out of here."

"No, you're not." Nassar flicks a piece of chewed crust off his robe. "They're gathering information on Azael, something you're incapable of doing inconspicuously."

"Does Pete know?" Chump's face turns beet red.

"He's busy," Nassar says.

"You don't have the authority…" Chump pauses, and the room goes silent.

"I'm in charge, and you have a job to finish." Nassar grabs a carton of pizza and a bottle of liquor, then he heads for the exit. "Get back to work. And under no circumstances is anyone else to leave this hotel."

Chapter 12

"**B**ULLSHIT." CHUMP picks up a couple fifty-pound barbells and curls alternating arms.

"He's a dick!" Javier adds, his head jutted toward the door.

Nassar seems content to let them have the last words because he's long gone while the men continue their insults.

I scan racks of weapons, fascinated. I'm safer handling the manila envelopes, preferring a paper cut to the deep laceration the sharp blades would inflict. My hope is that Chump will at least teach me to wield the Sword of Sin, but no one here seems to get along. With such a heavy armament, I'm surprised they haven't killed each other yet.

"We should be at the pub." Chump takes a swig of bourbon. "Demon surveillance is my job."

"Problem is, you don't survey them." Javier laughs. "You mutilate their slimy asses. That's why Pete wants you here. We need information, not body parts."

"Aren't demons unkillable?" I shove the rest of my pizza crust into my mouth.

"I don't execute 'em. I dismember 'em and bury the pieces separately across the San Isabel Mountain Range. Ulla makes a powder that's sprinkled in each of the holes to immobilize the limbs so they can't call out to each other."

"Demon extremities can communicate?" I cock my head and frown.

"Not with words. It's a psychic thing," Chump says. "If a hand digs free, it'll crawl any distance to collect and meld the body back together."

"Hmm…" I nod. "Good to know for when I take out Margery."

"Nice to meet you, tough guy. I'm Javier." The short guy laughs and turns two triangles of pizza into a sandwich before taking a huge bite.

"This place is insane," I say to change the subject. "Where did you get these weapons?"

"Lots of places over lots of years." Chump puts down the barbells.

"He brings the term "old bastard" to a new level," Javier says.

"Yeah, I've been around the block a few times, so what?" He jumps at his friend, pretends to strike a punch, and exhales like a bull.

Javier stands firm. "He's a real-life Viking. One of the first to land in North America."

"Viking?" My interest piques.

"It's a sore spot because he was left behind. That's when he met Margery and signed his soul over to Satan for a turkey leg and ear of corn."

"That part of me is a thousand years gone," he says. "Now, I mutilate demons and maintain the arsenal."

I pull a weapon with a long, lethally curved blade and a six-foot handle off the rack. The metal grip is cold as I balance the heavy end. "What is this? How is it used? Will it chop through Margery's neck?"

"Careful with the bardiche." Chump snatches it from me. "No touching the blades when you're drinking… except for me."

Throwing my hands up, I realize he's right. A third of the gin is missing from the bottle. While I'm not a lightweight, a reunion with Pete, sloshing drunk, is unwise.

"Let's sneak out and join Izi and the guys at the pub," Javier says. "Maybe we'll find Margery, and tough guy here can steal her troll hairdo next."

Word has spread fast about my absorption ability. They better not ask for a cigarette demonstration.

"Speaking of," I say, "does Izi have spiky black and white hair?"

"Yeah," Javier says. "You met her?"

"No. Passed her in the hall on the way here."

"Then you can meet her when we go to the pub." Chump places the bardiche back on the rack.

"Nah. I've caused enough trouble today. Besides, my contract with Satan's not fully broken. I've been told there are a lot of bounty hunters looking for me." I leave out that I should call my mom, not wanting them to think I'm a pussy. And that I want to be here to find out if Trisha tracked down Nina.

"C'mon," Javier begs. "There's plenty of time for a few shots before Pete and the others arrive. And the pub's a neutral zone. No one will mess with you there."

"I really have no energy to go anywhere," I say. "My room and a soft pillow await."

"Couriers don't need rest," they both say.

"Then why do I feel like I could sleep for three days?" Besides, a long winter's nap wouldn't prepare me for a second dose of the pancake antidote.

We laugh.

"I've got a better idea." Chump grins. "Let's go downstairs to the mystical defenses chamber."

"Mystical? Chamber?" I perk up.

"Weapons so magically powerful, they're locked up in a vault," Javier says. "The Sword of Sin is stored there. Want to see it?"

Even though I'm curious about the many wonders the room has to offer, I worry about them having another agenda. And I can't risk further pissing off Pete, Trisha… God. "Nassar wants the envelopes stuffed. I can do that if you guys want to leave. Show me how."

"Forget him," Javier says. "Trolling on Instagram with a bottle of booze will keep him occupied for hours."

"I don't know."

Javier mocks me in a whiny voice. "What are you, chicken? Bwak, bwak."

"We'll be in the vault fifteen minutes, tops," Chump says before the two men steer me out of the room.

Chapter 13

WHEN WE reach the exit sign I passed earlier, Javier opens the door and Chump grasps the back of my t-shirt. Considering this is where I encountered Izi and her crew, my uneasy feeling ignites into a fireball of dread. These guys must think I'm stupid.

"Where are we going?" My mind grapples with the possibilities. Is our destination the magical weapons room? Or is it more likely the pub? Worst-case scenario, they intend to turn me over to a bounty hunter for the reward money.

"We told you," Chump says and pushes me through the doorway and onto a stairwell landing.

"But this is where the others…" I drag my feet down a few concrete steps, then wait and tighten my grip on the metal railing, afraid they might toss me to the bottom.

"What's the matter?" Chump takes the lead.

Behind me, Javier does his chicken routine, the sound echoing in the stairwell.

"If you want to learn to use those weapons upstairs," Chump says, "you and me are going to spend a lot of time in the basement. You can come with me now or later."

I suck air and slowly descend to where the men push me through the first door on our right. Javier flips a light switch, and my body twitches along with the loud click.

Of all the places, we end up in the hotel's laundry. Six dryers line the wall opposite the door, five of which are tumbling loads of white sheets, their motors at a constant hum. And the space is warm and smells of fabric softener.

We proceed past a table for folding in the center of the room and a row of washers set for easy transfer between machines. As we approach the dryer with an 'Out of Order' sign taped over the heat settings, I half chuckle. "Was this a ploy to get me to do your laundry?"

Chump reaches into the side pocket of his cargo shorts and pulls out a handful of silver and gold coins, then picks out the only three silver ones. Now, I'm sure this is a trick, or worse, some sort of hazing. Whatever these guys have planned, they can count me out.

"Look at him." Javier points at me and laughs. "He's as white as the sheets in the dryers."

"Let me guess." Chump strokes his orange beard. "You've never jumped through a portal."

"Of course not." I cross my arms. "A week ago, good versus evil and angels and demons were fiction."

"Here." He holds out the three coins. "You want to make the offering?"

"Hell no." I throw up my hands and shuffle backward. "Last time I made an offering, a demon spine essence popped out of a soda machine."

Momentarily, they stare at each other before Javier snatches the money. "We're jumping to another location. That's all." He inserts the coins in the slot and opens the dryer. A rainbow of colors whirls inside a cloudy haze.

"Cool, huh?" Chump grabs my arm. "C'mon, you've gotta see it up close."

While he tugs me closer, I resist. The portal could be an ethereal meat grinder set on pulverizing my soul into hamburger for the CEO of Hell's lunch.

My shoes screech against the floor. "Pete won't like this."

"Forget Pete." Javier shoves me from behind and Chump's fingers dig into my skinny arm. I stand erect to avoid diving inside, using my height as leverage. But I'm no match against the Viking's strength and agility. He clotheslines my gut with his forearm, and I collapse forward, the air forced out of me. My curly hair's sucked toward the portal's mesmerizing swirl. While flailing my arms, cigarettes shoot from my palms, but there's no telling if the hexed butts hit their intended targets.

As I lose the battle, I'm thrown off balance and tumble headfirst into the sacrificial abyss. Ash and sparks mix with hues that transform into a solid gray fog.

I'm glad they skipped the wash cycle, but I'll kill the morons if I get out of this in one piece.

Chapter 14

Wɪᴛʜ ᴀ thud, my movement ceases. I hold out my hands and prepare for another drop, but I've somehow landed on a chair or tall stool. Down below, the floor is composed of a black nothingness that causes my head to spin. Good thing the seat feels fixed, but…

Where the hell am I?

I grip the edge of a bar top, recognizable because straight ahead, liquor bottles levitate in two horizontal rows.

Of course. The pub.

My gut burns. How could I have been so gullible again? Not that they gave me a choice. At least I'm not being roasted for Satan's dinner.

To my right, Chump slaps my back. "Wasn't such a terrible trip."

Javier laughs. "Thought we were sending you to Hell to collect the bounty, didn't ya?"

"Hilarious." I roll my eyes, but I'm still suspicious. These guys will do anything to get what they want. For once, I'd much rather be back at the hotel, doing what I'm told.

I cough, my breath stirring up ash that coats the surface of the metal bar where my glasses and twenty plus smoldering cigarettes landed. Scratching my head upsets more residue. How did I jump without lighting my hair on fire? Hopefully, the hexed butts taught them an electrifying lesson during our trip. Maybe they'll think twice before screwing with me in the future. More likely not.

"Listen, man," a chubby dark-haired bartender says in a brash voice, "smoke all you want, but for God's sake, use this." He flings a clear glass ashtray in my direction. Miraculously, I catch it against my chest.

"Sorry."

"Sorry," he mocks with air quotes. Then a blue sock and tattered tighty-whities drop out of nowhere and hit his head before falling on top of the mess. He closes his eyes and pulls at his hair with both hands, leaving it scruffy. His eyebrows dip into a demonic frown. "Who is this guy? He's disgusting."

"He's not so bad." Chump snatches the undergarments and shoves them in his pocket. "Clothes are mine. Lost 'em yesterday."

Interesting that he's sticking up for me. Also interesting that our server looks disturbingly familiar.

"Good Lord!" The bartender tugs at his belt, lifting his baggy jeans over his black button up shirt and to the base of his beer gut. "Empty the lint trap before you jump, so I don't have to look at your nasty drawers again. Otherwise, I'll charge extra for the trauma. Now, what do you dickheads want to drink?"

"Whiskey for me and Javier. Our friend likes gin." Chump pays with gold coins the size of pennies.

"Nothing for me," I say. "I'm not staying."

The bartender's quick to bark, "You pay every round whether or not you order."

"Bring another whiskey," Chump says.

As our server picks up the last coin, a cigarette on the counter pops and snaps. He jerks, retracting his hand. I cover my wide grin with my palm. The others avert their eyes.

"Clean up this fucking mess or I'll serve you a Virgin Mary!" The guy slams three shot glasses onto the metal surface, then spins around and retrieves a floating bottle with amber liquid.

My fingers jitter while I sweep the butts into the ashtray, but there's no reaction to my touch. Either they're depleted of magic or have identified their new master.

The bartender pours the first round of shots, spilling alcohol onto the remaining litter. Wet ash covers the side of my hand and smears the surface. I purse my lips and keep my opinion to myself.

"Who is he?" I whisper to Javier.

After the bartender walks away, he answers, "Comedian. Name's Ted Fielding, but you might be too young to recognize him. Died back in the eighties, at the prime of his career."

"Wait. I know him," I say. "He's in a film I love."

"Was in a lot of stuff," Chump says, "but no one can ever remember what."

"No, wait. I know it. It's on the tip of my tongue." I gawk at Fielding, star-struck, but no matter how hard I try, my memory fails me.

"You won't remember," Chump says. "The Earthbound Spirits' Pub is a neutral zone for otherworldly types, same as the Purgalator Coffee Shop. Souls in Limbo run the pub, and the bartenders are celebrities who've committed suicide or overdosed."

I shiver, remembering Margery used to send me on Purgalator coffee runs.

"They're given a choice to come here or go to Hell's Refugee Camp." Javier hops off his stool, leans against the bar, and balances on the bottomless abyss of a floor.

"Ted committed suicide," Chump says, "not that it'll help you remember his movies and TV shows. Everyone remembers the servers' names, but customers can never remember their accomplishments. Guess it's a preferable punishment than going to the refugee camp."

After a trip there, I'd push drinks too.

"I know you're concerned," Javier says, "but God's and Satan's forces can't hunt here. All patrons are required to keep the peace."

"Sucks," Chump says. "Nothin' funner than a good brawl every now and then."

By the sound of Chump's opinion of this place, keeping the peace is more of a suggestion. With any luck, we'll keep our visit low-key. No telling what might happen if I'm recognized as Hell's most wanted, even if the pub's neutral.

"The coins offered at the dryer were for Fielding's section," Chump says while using his index finger to draw boobs in the wet residue. He admires his artwork with a chuckle and adds, "He takes care of ex-couriers."

"Really? He's kind of an asshole." Then again, I'm sitting between two pricks who shoved me through a portal against my will.

Chump picks up a glass and exposes veins, bulging on his twenty-inch bicep. He downs the shot of whiskey, then snatches up the one in front of me, liquid spilling over his thumb. "Here's to living another night with our heads."

With a pretend glass in hand, I motion to swig the air whiskey. Javier savors his spirits with dainty sips. After a deep breath, I spin around and notice a wall of decorative mirrors, hanging midair and willy-nilly in the darkness, drifting like the bottles. Oddly, the glass reflects the bar's furnishings and other objects in the place, but we patrons are invisible, as if we're vampires. Or it's how the pub assures anonymity, not that it's giving me a warm fuzzy that no one will recognize me.

A stream of color whooshes through a gold-leaf frame and targets a barstool a few seats down from where Javier stands. It solidifies into a demon with alligator skin. An orange glow radiates from the cracks over his face and neck and hands. The rest of him is covered in a black tracksuit with white stripes trimming the legs and sleeves.

Explains our transport into this place, the mounts being the portals, but how do I make the exit offering to slide back to the laundry room?

The hunched over demon tosses a gold coin onto the bar, and Fielding glides in with a blue flaming froufrou drink. When Tracksuit turns and stares though glowing eyes on a hairless gorilla-like face, I divert my attention to the opposite side of the room.

There are quite a few demon patrons, and the pub extends farther than the eye can see. With Satan's bounty hunters on the prowl, the dim setting is welcome, unless our new neighbor has recognized me.

"How big is the pub?" I ask. "And why is it so chilly?"

"Who knows? Who cares?" Chump motions for a refill.

"It's Limbo," Javier says, "not a warm day at Disneyland."

When I turn to face the demon, he's still looking at me.

I ask the guys, "How do we return to the hotel?"

"Too many questions," Chump says.

"Hey, this place may be neutral, but I doubt it applies to someone with a warrant for damnation and a father like…" I snap my mouth shut when Fielding glides in, not wanting him to know my kinship to an escaped fallen angel.

The bartender sloppily pours our second round and says, "Crazy ex-courier alkies and your bottomless glasses."

"Speaking of drunks, Izi should be nearby." Javier takes a few steps backward and scans the area. His body bobs as if he's on a trampoline.

"Seen Izi and her crew?" Chump asks Fielding.

"Tracking your stupid friends isn't in my job description." Fielding glares at me. "I hope you wipe your ass cleaner than you scrubbed my bar."

I straighten and bounce a knee.

Chump leans back and checks out my butt. "Don't see any flies."

Fielding flings a rag at me. The cold dampness slaps my face before falling into my lap. I get to work, polishing the surface while biting my tongue.

"Izi must be here somewhere." Javier shifts closer to the decorated frames. "Guess I'll go find them."

"Hey, wait!" But he's already out of sight.

I motion to follow him until Fielding slaps the bar and yells, "Finish your job."

"Okay, okay." I wipe faster, my intent to discover a way out of here rising.

Chapter 15

"Javier'll be right back." Chump guzzles the shots in front of us.

"I'm guessing your liquor tolerance is high," I say.

"Who are you, my mother?"

"Listen, you guys can stay, but I've had a miserable day. I just want to go back to the hotel." I try to sound casual because they have given me no reason to trust them. Maybe Javier's looking for Izi and her crew. Maybe he's off to find a bounty hunter.

"Stop being such a pussy." He grabs Javier's unfinished drink, toasts with my forehead and turns up a grin. Whiskey splashes onto the bridge of my nose. The sweet smell has my tongue out to capture a drip.

I scan down Chump's side of the bar, hoping to catch a glimpse of someone leaving. If he won't clue me in, I'll figure an exit route on my own.

On the opposite side of the bar, Tracksuit and I make eye contact again. He snarls, then returns to his drink, swallowing flames and all.

Worried the demon might identify me, I nudge Chump.

"What now?"

"Don't look, but the goon a few seats over recognizes me."

"Stop being paranoid. Probably likes your girlish figure."

"Seriously, he keeps staring." I wiggle in my seat. "I've got to get out of here."

"Calm down." Chump pulls a three-inch switchblade with a wood-stained handle out of his pocket. The blade snaps to attention, and he starts to clean his nails.

"Put that away," I whisper and nudge his arm.

"Grow a pair," he says, "or you won't last long in this world."

Tracksuit calls over in a scratchy voice, "You're Barry, Barry White Frost." He pulls folded paper from his pocket and shakes it open. It's a warrant for damnation with my face, front and center, proclaiming I'm wanted in Hell, preferably with my head detached.

"You think that's him?" Chump snickers. "You need glasses."

Tracksuit says, "I'd bet money—"

Chump slams a shot glass on the metal surface. His eyes narrow in on the demon while he raises the blade.

All the reasons to avoid this place replay in my head. With no escape plan, I rub the back of my neck and pray Chump doesn't make the situation worse.

The bartender moves in and leans over the bar where Javier was sitting. "What in the living hell…?"

"Mind your own business," the demon says.

"Don't tell me what to do. This is a safe zone. Keep the peace, or I'll launch everyone to Siberia." Fielding snatches the wanted poster from the goon, crumples it over his head, and throws it backward. Then he points at Chump. "You know better than to enter the pub armed."

He closes the knife and puts it in his pocket.

"Nice try." Fielding holds out his chubby palm. "That's mine."

"No way, it's the only one I brought."

Our bartender persists, wiggling his fingers, his expression sour.

"Stupid rules." Chump digs the knife out and hands it over.

The tracksuit demon laughs and slaps a silver coin on the bar. Two seconds later he's a streak of black, white, and orange, sucked through the frame where he entered.

While I'm glad the creepy goon's gone, and he showed me how to exit this place, there's no chance he'll give up on my bounty.

Chapter 16

"**I**F A demon with a wanted poster featuring me doesn't convince you that we need to leave, I don't know what will," I say.

Chump slumps over the bar. "We're not getting out without Javier."

"Why?"

"He's got our exit offerings."

"Why's he holding the coins? What about the change in your pocket?"

"That's for drinks," he says. "Javier doesn't trust me to get us out of here because I've lost all our money in bets."

"So, your motto is, 'What happens in Vegas keeps you homeless in Vegas?'"

"Look at you," Chump says, "saving humanity one joke at a time."

I glance upward into the dark abyss, downward into nothingness, then over my shoulder at the ornately framed mirrors. "Any other way to leave this place?"

"Sure, if you don't mind a bartender ousting you to a location of his choice. Fielding already threatened to send us to Siberia. Piss him off some more, and he'll launch you to the Arctic Circle or Sahara Desert. You want to risk that?"

"You're kidding?"

"Fielding once cast me onto a fishing boat in the middle of Lake Michigan. Took me a week to return to Trinidad." Chump waves an empty shot glass at the bartender. "Anyway, we've gotta be here to jump to where we entered. How it works."

My heart races and my thoughts search for a solution. "What if I borrow an exit coin?"

"Finding a generous patron in this place could take hours, hell, days. And it's not the best way to stay incognito."

I drum my fingers on the bar.

"Chill out. I'm sure Javier will be back any minute with Izi and her crew."

Fielding glides in with a bottle of whiskey and pours three refills.

"Don't worry so much. Have a drink." Chump throws more gold coins on the bar, lifts his seventh shot, and motions to toast before downing it.

Maybe he's right. I snatch a glass, then gulp and gasp. But I regret taking the drink because I'll need to keep pace with Chump to calm *my* nerves. Having an exit offering in hand would do the same.

I tilt my chair backward and wonder what would happen if I'm captured. Would bounty hunters deliver me directly to the CEO of Hell? And what manner of torture would Satan inflict?

Shit!

"I'm going to find Javier," I say.

"There's no telling how far down the bar he might be. Do you really want to expose yourself to dozens more demons?"

"You said this is a safe zone." I scan the direction where Javier headed, but he's nowhere to be seen.

"That's right," he says. "You're the one who's paranoid, but it's your time to waste."

"Yes, it is." And I might stay if it weren't for all his mixed messages.

I spin around, hop off the stool, and land on a springy floor. Chump clutches my arm, but I pull away and drop to one knee on the darkness. Onlookers laugh and I blush.

"Don't be so sensitive," Chump says. "Happens to everyone the first time they stand here."

After a few wobbly test steps, I flip him the bird and follow Javier's path.

"Shit," Chump yells. "Come back here!"

Chapter 17

MY SEARCH for Javier slows behind a half dozen bright green beings with heads as pointy and curved as a rhinoceros' horn. They're all wearing sparkly, tight-fitted dresses and appear to be celebrating demon girls' night out. Their hips sway to a fluty sound that resonates from the group. The more the siren song plays, the more my stride involuntarily synchronizes with the tune. Disturbed by what might happen next, I cover my ears.

The tallest one turns and looks me up and down with beady black eyes set near her thick neck. She strokes her horny head, taps the sharp tip, and says something inaudible.

"What?" I uncover my ears.

She winks. "Bend over, Cutie."

My ass cheeks clench as her friends close in. "No thanks." I twirl to guard against horns and duck into an empty spot at the bar. Lucky for me, they have short attention spans and regroup to search for another victim. After they're gone, I recognize Javier standing off to the right. He's between a Minotaur and a crowded seating area where Margery's hosting Izi and her crew.

Fuck!

I lean against the bar, hoping to go unnoticed while my mind floods with questions.

Chump catches up and squeezes in beside me.

"You set me up." I pound my fist on the bar.

He frowns and scratches his temple, but I don't buy his puzzled look.

"Is that Javier and Izi with…" I point at the group. "Margery?"

"Shhhit," he says, long and drawn out.

"What did that demon bitch offer you guys to bring me here?"

"No way, man. We'd never strike a deal with Margery." The pucker in his bushy auburn brow deepens. "Javier's being held hostage."

Sure, he's struggling against the Minotaur, who is likely named Bruno. Their kind all look alike, and Margery owns a herd of the beasts. Bruno abducted Nina last night, so I'm prepared to settle a grudge.

"You forced me here," I say, "and tried to prevent me from coming down here. Sure seems like you've been lying—"

"Stop." Chump holds up his hand. "We only came to the pub to fuck with Nassar. And we've been screwing with you because you deserved a little hazing after the trouble you've caused today."

No matter his excuse, it still feels like he's covering something up. "Explain Izi and her crew at that table with our ex-boss."

"Can't." He stares at a clenched fist, shaking near his chest.

"Assuming we *are* on the same side, what do we do now?"

Chump pulls a knife out of his pocket. His expression turns wild. "I grind the Minotaur into hamburger and free Javier, then we run to our seats and present the exit offering."

No surprise, he lied about not having an arsenal in his pants, but I'm thankful regardless. While scanning behind the bar for Fielding, I pray he hasn't seen the weapon, but instead find Amy Morgan pouring drinks. Again, I recognize her name, and that she's a singer, but none of her songs comes to mind. *Not important.*

Worried Chump's blood thirst will cause more trouble, I say, "No. This *is* a neutral zone, and we should use that to our advantage. I'll move in and draw attention to Margery holding Javier against his will. Maybe, just maybe, she'll let him go."

Chump snort and tugs on his beard. "When that doesn't work, I'll grind the Minotaur into hamburger."

I sigh, agreeing there's a slim chance she'll release him. "Please. No carnage. Let's do this without risking an eternal ban from the pub."

He nods, but it's highly unlikely we'll escape this place without him pulverizing someone or something.

With my palms up, a yellow glow forms in the center. "Worst case, I'll turn Margery's own wrath on her and the Minotaur."

"Sweet." He grins. "Lighting up that bitch with her own cigarettes is worth waiting to see."

"Creep up near Javier but wait for my signal before attacking."

"One more thing," Chump says. "Don't get too close to Margery. She can make an offering and jump with you to a location of her choice. I don't want to tell Pete she kidnapped you."

I rub the back of my neck, the heat in my hand soothing the tension. "*Geeze.* This is getting complicated. Anything else I should know about entering and exiting this place?"

"Nope." He puts the knife in his side pocket, giving the impression he'll cooperate.

"Ready?" I ask.

"I'm always ready." Chump stumbles toward Javier and sneaks behind a group of soldier apparitions that appear to have died in the Civil War. Does he realize everyone can see him through the ghosts? With my luck, Chump's whiskey binge is kicking in and his better judgment is checking out. Or worse, he doesn't care who sees him.

Chapter 18

MARGERY SHOVES a cigarette between her puckered lips and strikes a match on the table. Odd that she's smoking like a human. Still odder that I hold her cursed cigarettes in *my* hands.

Sweat seeps from my pits as I strut over and force a sarcastic laugh. "Lose something?" I focus on the warmth building in my palms.

She drops the flaming match, and it snuffs out on the infinite floor. "Look who's here," she says in her raspy voice. "Can't stay away from me, can you, Honey?"

"You wish." I lift an eyebrow and zero in on the tattooed woman. "Shocked to see me, Izi? Yeah, I know who you guys are. Care to explain why you're fraternizing with the enemy?"

Izi remains wide-eyed and speechless.

"They work for me again and have sworn allegiance to Azael." Margery points at the traitors, squirming in their seats. "Everyone, make room for Prince Moron."

"No thanks," I say. "Considering this place is a neutral zone, *Javier* and I won't be staying."

"Ha!" Javier struggles to escape the Minotaur's grip. "Told you they wouldn't desert me."

A growl builds in Margery's throat. She pokes the unlit cigarette at our lost crew. "You've signed your contracts. What are you waiting for? Jump your asses to the warehouse."

"What's the matter?" I ask. "Worried they'll change their minds and leave with me?"

"Someone thinks he's important." Her cackle turns evil, progressing to a snort mixed with an emphysema cough, the sound of which always makes me cringe.

"Laugh while you can, you old hag." I scratch my palms with my middle fingers to stifle a premature cigarette strike. Better to hit her when I can do the most damage.

The defectors fumble to slap silver coins on the table and disappear through a frame directly above. Amazing how they still fear her despite my absorbing her ability to torture humans. I'm glad there are three fewer obstacles to freeing Javier, but it's shocking they've entered a contract with the demon bitch twice. Doing so also implies they have little to no faith in me.

Margery crosses legs covered in shiny blue spandex pants, rests an elbow over the back of the chair, and snatches the unlit cigarette from between her nicotine-stained teeth. "Honey, you're wasting your time, playing with Pete and his insignificant cohorts. Let's tally. Father Timothy and a dozen nuns are dead. Three crew members are working for me again. Five more minutes, and I'll resign—"

Javier wrestles the Minotaur and yells, "I'd cut off my own head and go to Hell's Refugee Camp before I'd submit to you again!"

"Call off your goon." I stand frozen, jaw tight, palms burning.

"Or you'll what?" She draws on the cigarette, forgetting it's not lit, then blows out a smokeless breath.

Am I making her nervous?

"I'll light you up." I grunt and discharge a cigarette into my hand. So much for hitting her with a surprise attack. I show it to her between a thumb and index finger.

"You stole my cigs!" Her eyes turn black.

"Uh, huh." I smirk. "Suggest you release Javier or I'll—"

"Hit me with my own hex?" She lifts off her chair with her arms spread and spits the unlit dud to the side. "Go ahead, Honey. Give it a try."

While darting the cigarette, I hesitate and wonder why she's unfazed by my threat. Is she bluffing?

"Throw it!" Javier yells. "Light her ass on fire!"

On impulse, I do it. I pitch it. But the thing's got a mind of its own, altering my aim and settling on her puckered lip.

Crap!

I take a step back and brace myself for her wrath.

Margery draws in a long breath, burning half the cigarette to ash. She looks content, which seems wrong for a demon. Slowly, she blows a familiar lasso of smoke. The last time she caught me in a noose, I was paralyzed and pissed my pants. No chance I'm getting trapped in that again.

Defenseless and certain the demon bitch won't comply with the pub's neutral zone policies, I holler, "Chump!"

He's quick to intervene, storming through the soldier apparitions to stabs the Minotaur's thick forearm with three strikes. The beast swats him like a fly toward the bar, at the same time bugling so loud every being within sight turns to watch the brawl, including the pop-singer bartender.

Damn!

Please don't oust us. Please don't oust us.

With an arm loose and the Minotaur struggling to regain control, Javier digs into his pocket. "Get Chump out of here," he says to me, throwing two offering coins in my direction.

Miraculously, I catch one, but the other bounces off the table and lands near Margery's feet. Having accomplished only a third of our mission to return to the hotel, I regret not starting with Chump's plan to storm in and take no prisoners.

"Bruno! Get him out of here!" Margery darts the butt at the bull's head before she returns it to her mouth and inhales another whammy. She's hopping mad. Sparks rise from her spiky updo and bounce the other exit offering in the opposite direction.

While the Minotaur exits the pub, dragging Javier through the mirror that took the others, Chump belly flops onto the floor and crawls along the infinite surface to retrieve the loose coin. A good thing, because there's no quick path for me around the lasso of smoke that's heading for my neck.

With one hand, Chump snatches his offering; with the other, he stabs the demon bitch's foot. Then he releases a sadistic laugh that makes Margery's cackle sound like a giggling schoolgirl.

Damn! He's got balls.

Margery hops on her good foot and curses the day she met me. A black smog veils her head, and she freezes in place.

Did she jinx herself?

My question is answered when she teeters and falls face down on the floor.

"Run!" Chump jumps up and serpentines around the smoke.

We've lost Javier, but now is our only window to escape before that cigarette hex wears off and Margery towers over us with giant claws and teeth.

Chump and I dash toward our portal, him taking the lead while I totter on the unstable floor. I clutch my exit offering so tightly it could melt in the palm of my hand.

But there's a problem when we reach our section of the bar.

Tracksuit is sitting in Chump's spot. In mine, the scariest looking dude I've ever seen.

And behind us, the smoke lasso and a ten-foot Margery are in pursuit.

Chapter 19

Tracksuit's eyes widen when he spots us. He nudges the scary trench coat-clad caveman sitting beside him.

With a black pinky fingernail, the caveman picks at the rotting teeth buried inside his overgrown auburn facial hair. Even fifteen feet away, the man smells like he showers once a century and is a decade overdue.

"What now?" I turn to Chump, figuring he can take the big dirty guy, but what might heading off with a fire eating demon do to me?

"Prepare for pain." He blows out a long breath, fluffing his mustache. "That's Roy Morrow in the coat, a mercenary who works for the highest bidder. There's no doubt he's here for you."

Not what I wanted to hear. I peer over my shoulder. "He'll collect nothing if that smoke lasso or Margery catches us first."

"This is going to be tricky." Chump scratches his forehead, then lifts an index finger. "Shoot one of those hexed butts. Hurry. Fielding's not looking."

I discharge a cigarette at Roy, but he holds his ground. His unibrow dips into a frown as he wipes ash from his lapel. The smoldering cigarette falls to the floor.

"Got a better idea?"

Chump calls toward the bar, "Hey, Fielding, I thought this place is neutral. What's a mercenary doing in our seats?"

I hope no one realizes I'm their target.

Fielding moves in, his whole body shaking as he yells at Tracksuit, "I warned you!"

Roy crosses his arms under his beard, appearing to have no intentions of moving. A long Egyptian-style sword peeks out from beneath his trench coat. Good to know he follows rules as well as Chump.

"Get out or I'll launch you all to Siberia." Fielding pulls the soda fountain gun from beneath the bar and sprays seltzer at the interlopers' heads.

Roy snarls, snatches the soda gun with his sausage fingers and takes a turn shooting Fielding's face. The bartender steps backward, his mouth tight, and wipes his face like Mo in the *Three Stooges*.

This is getting ugly. Fielding's probably seconds away from ousting his entire section. The sooner we're back in the laundry room, the better.

Chump whispers in my ear to try a cigarette on the demon, so I zing a few at Tracksuit, hoping to at least knock him off his feet. Instead, his left arm breaks off at the shoulder joint and falls onto the floor.

"Did that just happen?" I cover my mouth and laugh.

"Follow my lead… and hurry." Chump kicks the limb aside and the demon dives for it. With a path cleared, he rushes the bar and slams a coin on the metal surface. Nearby, a mirror with a silver frame sucks him in.

The smoke lasso and Margery close in, her enormous feet tripping over the wavy floor. I've no choice but to slip my offering in beside Roy, launching me next.

A pressure squeezes my ankle. I'm tugged and tossed through pops of light, making me dizzy. While twirling out of control, I worry the lasso is yanking me in reverse. Or Margery's trying to snap my legs like a wishbone.

Finally, I land, half hanging out of the dryer, my glasses on the floor.

"What are you doing?" Chump frowns.

"Is the dryer spinning?"

"Of course not." He chuckles, lifts the back of my pants, and drops me onto the floor. "Maybe the trip cooked your brain."

"Could be." I groan. "Feels like my head's going to explode."

"My ride was fine." He points at my leg. "Maybe it's that."

The lasso jumped, as suspected, around my ankle. I kick my foot over the dissipating smoke and pick up my glasses.

"Or him!" Chump lifts his finger to the dryer's circular opening.

Tracksuit demon dangles from the hole.

I roll to the side and shoot cigarettes that light up the area. He retaliates by throwing his dismembered arm at me, the hand reaching to grab my neck.

"Run!" Chump shouts, but I'm already on my feet, close behind him.

In the rear, our pursuer screams, "Get back here! Your bounty is mine… all mine."

As I ascend the steps two at a time and shoot butts behind me, I'm afraid to check if any have hit the demon or lit the place on fire. As we reach the main floor, Chump throws open the door, and we continue our escape toward the lobby.

"Fig! Get my machete!" Chump hollers, then adds, "Barry, keep running. Past the desk. To the entry."

When we round the corner, he reaches his hand out and catches the weapon as if they've been practicing for this moment their whole lives.

I pass them as ordered, but the sound of a sharp edge slicing through flesh piques my curiosity. I put on the brakes and slam into the glass door. Facing the check-in desk, I fumble to put on my glasses, then watch the decapitated demon hit the floor with a thud. Kind of amazing, he was able to reattach his arm, a thing Chump had warned about. His head rolls near the hallway that leads to the rooms, but halts and reverses direction. Another lesson in how demons reassemble.

"Got him." Fig runs and collects the head by the ears, holding the face outward. The demon's mouth opens and closes, the slithery tongue wagging with a gurgle. And his eyes have rolled back in the sockets.

"Surprised he's not spitting fire balls," Chump says.

"Me too." Fig edges behind the check-in desk.

"Huh?" I close in on the body and gag at the sight of the smoldering, bright-orange blood that snakes from the demon's neck and across the tile floor. It's the same color that emitted from his alligator-like skin back at the bar.

"When you decapitate a fire eater," he says, "he'll strike with what's left of the fuel on his tongue."

I stare down at the bastard, remembering how he sipped a flaming drink. A defensive fuel of sorts, I suppose.

Fig returns carrying the head inside a burlap sack. In the other hand, she's clutching a pile of additional bags. She drops them beside Chump, along with the head, then runs away like a nervous bird. "Back in a second with the twine."

"Come here." Chump waves me in closer to where he's kneeling near the demon's legs. "Careful, don't step in the blood. It will heat up the soles of your shoes and burn your feet. Once that shit gets on your skin, it'll blister like a mother for days."

"How can I help?" I tiptoe around the flow of gore.

"Hit his arm with a cigarette again." He points at the shoulder joint.

I shoot, and the limb detaches as cleanly as it did at the pub. At first, I grin, thinking this is a handy ability, then realize Margery could have done this to me.

"Perfect." Chump grabs a burlap sack and shoves the arm inside. "Fig! Where are those ties?"

"Coming." She returns, transitioned into a man, carrying shiny silver twine. Fig goes to work on the bag with the head inside, first twirling it closed, then tying a cord around the cinched spot. Chump does the same with the next sack. The ties meld, creating a smooth and permanent restraint.

"Pop off the other arm," he says.

Fig claps, witnessing the cigarette in action, then says in a deep voice, "Perfect, no blood."

"Pretty cool, huh?" Chump turns to me. "Now do the legs."

But off to one side, the fingers wriggle on the detached arm, crawling and dragging itself toward the shoulder. The demon's skin stretches, trying to meld together.

"Oh no you don't." Chump whistles a tune while he grabs the limb and shoves it into another sack. He hands the bag to Fig, who seals it with more of the magical twine.

"Whoa," I say, amazed by the entire process, but also thankful the arm won't require a third removal. They're enjoying this, but I'm not. With each subsequent strike, there's an unsettling rush that makes me hesitate. Could this be what Margery feeds on when she delivers a blistery punishment?

"Don't just stand there," he says, "take off the other leg. Then try to break the torso in half."

"I'll get a mop and clean up the blood from the neck." Fig rushes toward the hallway. "Do you need more sacks or twine?"

"No." Chump straddles the sack and ties it like a cowboy competing in an evil rodeo.

With a palm aimed at the second leg, the entryway door opens. Pete and Candy walk in, followed by at least a dozen nuns.

"Uh oh." I drop my hand, afraid of what they'll think, but I'm equally relieved to see them alive.

"Kissamyass." Candy slaps bare feet on the tile. "Told you something didn't feel right. I should've come here sooner."

Ulla and Inez emerge from the crowd and collect the cigarettes from the floor. "Better hope this demon breach hasn't compromised the hotel."

Chapter 20

PETE PACES while pinching his lower lip. Every few steps he twitches, and a shiny black strand of hair bounces. I'd hate to hear the conversation he's having with Boss in his head.

"Is this the only breach?" Candy places her hands on her ample hips, cinching her shirt stained with blood.

"Yes." Chump stands to face her. "This could have been a lot worse."

"Bullshit!" Candy's screeches, "This hotel is supposedly protected from evil, but there's a demon in it. My gut says this is way worse than it looks."

Pete intervenes. "Candy, we don't have time for debates. Escort the nuns to Nassar's room, and I'll assess the damage."

"Why me?" she says. "I'm Barry's babysitter. If I had been watching him, this never would have happened."

The nun with the large nose and soft voice turns to Pete, her short gray veil swaying against her shoulders. "It would be good for the sisters to watch them prepare a demon for burial."

Chump points at the demon's groin. I take it as an invitation to shoot a cigarette at the remaining leg, and the limb breaks loose. "Pretty cool, huh?" he says.

Gawking nuns in blood spattered gray pants, sweater vests, and white-collared shirts, huddle and whisper and squeal.

"Pete!" Candy says. "This is turning into a free-for-all!"

"Next demon burial, Sister Theresa." Pete's tremors migrate through his entire body. Besides Candy's objection, his demon could be freaking out, seeing one of its own chopped into pieces. "Please, off to Nassar's room."

"Follow me, sisters." Candy waves the group toward the entry to the rooms. The sisters shuffle backward on their black Skechers, gawking at us. They seem to be ready for a demon hunt of their own.

As they disappear around the corner, one asks, "Can we go to Chump's room instead?"

"Oh yes," another says. "We want to see the weapons."

Pete stares at the ceiling and shakes his head. "Keeping those holy women in line is like herding cats."

Chump laughs. "They could kick all our asses."

"Really?" I say.

"Three of them are Daughters of Light," Pete says. "Sister Theresa is the Reverend Mother and two are teachers. The other half dozen are skilled fighters, like ninjas. If it weren't for them, Azael would have taken off with a few new wives."

"Were there any mummy couriers at the convent?" I ask Pete.

"Azael tore through the entryway with skaks, but the nuns beheaded them while your father flew away to bombard us at the boarding house." He puts his fingers in his pockets. "Now tell me what happened here?"

"We jumped to the Earthbound Spirit's Pub," I say. "This demon piggybacked onto my return trip."

"Weren't you told to stay here?" Pete says.

"Yes, but…" I waver, careful with my words, knowing everyone is tired of my excuses. And blaming Chump and Javier will only cause more tension. Plus, I'm starting to like them. "We only went for a quick shot."

"Because the crate of liquor I had delivered wasn't enough?" Pete's nostrils flare.

"It was my decision." Chump stands, chest out. "Besides, we got some—"

"Shocking news," I say, "and you won't be happy."

"Everything that's happened today has been a pain in my ass," Pete says. "Why would I expect good news?"

"Go ahead. Tell him," Chump says, "but first shoot the demon in half."

"Sure." Just as expected, the cigarette does the job, along with sending a surge up my spine.

"That's a nifty trick, but how'd you get to this point." Pete rubs his brow.

I bite my lip before blurting out, "We followed Izi and her guys to the pub."

"Wait a minute. My express instructions were for everyone to stay here."

Nassar swaggers into the room, wagging his finger. His red silk robe hangs open, exposing a wife beater t-shirt and plaid boxers. "You better not be blaming me for this."

Candy jogs to catch up, carrying a long, wrapped rope made of red licorice. She's changed into a pair of UGG boots with fur around the ankles, completely inappropriate for a hot June day, but nothing Candy does is ordinary.

"Nassar," Pete says, "would you care to explain why you let them leave the hotel?"

"Izi worked extra hard, finishing her crew's set of leases. She said they'd be gone for an hour, tops, and could collect information. Besides, she's dependable, unlike this one." Nassar pokes Chump's arm with a French manicured fingernail.

Chump shoves him. "If Izi's so trustworthy, why were she and her guys there with Margery, abandoning us?"

"Kissamyass!" Candy's eyes pop while she removes the crinkly wrapper from her licorice. She takes a bite and stares, like she's watching a horror movie.

Pete glares at me. "They what?"

"He's right. They defected." I look at the floor. "And we lost Javier too."

"Not surprised Javier deserted us." Nassar puts a hand on his hip.

"He would never go back to Margery!" Chump growls. "The evil bitch kidnapped him."

"Well, I know nothing about this." Nassar huffs and points at me. "It's time to lay blame where it belongs. Barry's been a problem since he started working for Margery. None of this would be happening if the Catholic Church hadn't let a Nephilim live."

Who is this guy blaming everything on me? While there's no denying I've done selfish things, he has no idea what I've been through this week.

"Enough," Pete calls out. "We've known about Barry for years, and we've all accepted this mission unconditionally. At least I thought we had."

"I won't be silent," Nassar says. "In twenty-four hours, we've lost nearly everything. We're better off fighting Azael without Barry."

A burning in my gut intensifies. I approach him, my mouth open, ready to tell him to leave if he doesn't trust me. Instead, an orange flame shoots out and over Nassar's face and chest.

Crap.

Chapter 21

Nassar freezes with his eyes closed. His skin is singed, and his facial hair is burned off.

I brush his scorched robe and lisp with a blazing tongue. "So sorry. The demon. When he piggybacked. I must have acquired—"

"Stop it." Nassar slaps my hand. "It's ruined."

Chump's bent over laughing. Candy grins, exposing a mouth full of red licorice. I'm starting to wonder how she still has teeth.

"This isn't funny." Pete steps between us. "Nassar, go see Ulla and Inez."

Nassar pivots on a black patent-leather pump, and a small flame fizzling out at his shoulder. "If I scar…"

"This absorption ability of yours," Pete says, "it's becoming a huge problem."

"But it's pretty fucking cool." Chump moves closer. "Open your mouth."

"No." Pete pulls him away from my face. "Keep your distance until we figure out how Barry robs others of their abilities."

"Where's Trisha?" I try to lick my lips with a dry tongue. "She should be in on this."

"Right here." There's a sharp poke to my arm.

I jump. "Don't do that."

Trisha taps a toe, expressing her irritation. "Barry, this is getting ridiculous, all the trouble you're causing. Why didn't you stay here like you promised? I'm ready to put a leash on you… make you my pet."

"You know what happened at the pub?" My brow lifts.

"It's headline news in Purgatory." She focuses on the bagged limbs and the remaining half torso. "I didn't want to believe you kidnapped a demon, but here's the evidence."

"Satan thinks I kidnapped that?" I point at the remains and push my glasses up my nose. "More like he tried to capture *me* for the bounty."

"Whether you're guilty or not," Trisha says, "abduction has been added to your warrant for damnation."

Great.

"Where are the nuns?" Trisha cocks her head.

"In Nassar's room," Candy says.

"Hopefully they haven't settled in, because this place has been compromised."

"Seriously?" Pete glares at me.

With hands on her hips, Trisha says, "One hundred percent. Satan knows Barry is his nephew and is more determined than ever to capture him. Because this demon was able to enter the hotel, the other bounty hunters are headed here. Even if they don't find a way in, they'll wait us out. We need to move everyone to my cave before they arrive.

"Not a chance, bitch." Pete's face spasms. He clamps a hand over his mouth.

"Was that his demon?" I nudge Chump, who's on his knees, stuffing the remaining piece of torso into a burlap bag. He confirms with a nod.

Trisha moves in, nose-to-nose with Pete. "Well, well, Boss. For once, you talk for yourself."

Red spots expand on Pete's arm, where he continues to scratch, and his voice wavers as he says, "Azael took over your cave the year Barry was born. Unless you've found a way to protect against a fallen angel break-in again, Boss has reason for concern."

"After I put Azael back in his tomb," Trisha says, "the archangels fortified the cave. Frankly, Poison Canyon's the safest place nearby, and our only option. Let's pack it up and get out of here ASAP."

"Is that where Nina is?" I ask.

"Yes." Trisha forces a smile.

Candy rolls her eyes and changes the subject. "How are we transporting everyone to your cave? Assuming Trisha got the Hummer back, we only have three SUVs to transport a dozen nuns and the rest of us, not to mention the weapons and supplies we'll be moving."

"Those vehicles are risky, so I've brought a junk truck." Trisha turns to me and explains. "They're how God transports divine objects and hides evil relics. There are multiple junk trucks that carry all cargo at all times, but none of it at any time."

"That doesn't make sense," I say.

"Oh, no, it's brilliant." Candy's face lights up. "I've heard about them, but thought they were a myth."

"It's simple," Trisha says. "Any of God's collectables can be in any of the trucks at any given time. If you discover a truck and intend to steal something inside, it will disappear. Just be aware that anyone searching for us will never locate us inside the junk truck, nor will they see the junk truck once we're moving."

I nod but still don't understand what she's describing. Maybe I will when I'm in one.

Candy shoves her licorice in her bra and shuffles toward the entrance to our assigned rooms. "I'll gather the nuns and the weapons."

"Haul them to the basement exit," Trisha calls out. "The junk truck is parked there."

"Hey, that's my arsenal," Chump says. "I should be in charge of moving 'em."

"No. Finish packaging that demon." Pete seems to have snapped out of his Boss-induced trance but continues to work at his itch. "Do your thing and hide him in the mountains as quickly as possible."

"Meet me at the sand dunes when you're done," Trisha tells Chump. "I need help to map out Margery's encampment and figure out where Azael is hiding."

Chump smiles. "Can Barry come with me? I want to show him how to dispose of a demon."

"You guys have caused enough trouble," Pete snaps back, his violet pupils dilated.

"Besides," Trisha says, "Barry's warrant is too sought after. He's the most important thing we'll hide in the junk truck."

"If we find Javier," Chump says, "can I free him from Margery?"

"No," she says. "There's no time, and we don't want to draw attention."

Chump ties the last burlap sack and curses under his breath.

"Get it together, everyone," Trisha says. "We've got to be out of here in thirty minutes." She turns to me. "Follow me downstairs to visit Ulla and Inez. You need another dose of the contract antidote."

"And I'm assuming you still need to call your mother," Pete says.

"Bleck," I say, but I'm not sure which leaves a worse taste in my mouth.

Chapter 22

TEN MINUTES later, in the closet-sized apothecary in the basement, I down the last of the antidote and slam the tall cup on the counter. There's nowhere to make pancakes, so I gagged my way through the old bug-filled brew. It's a tossup if the bitter aftertaste or the lingering fishy odor is worse.

I let out a loud burp as Candy enters with helper nuns in the rear. A few of them wave the stink away from their noses. "Sorry." I raise my palm.

Candy holds her nose. "This better mean your lazy ass finally finished."

"Yes," I belch in her face on purpose.

She blinks and motions to punch me in the stomach but stops short of my jutted gut. I hold firm, knowing she wouldn't dare risk a face full of bugs and eyeballs from upchucked antidote.

She picks up the folded metal exam table resting against the wall. "You should have downed it faster."

"Easier said than done." I glare at her, an eyebrow raised.

"We need all hands on deck to empty this place." The nuns follow Candy's lead, scurrying to collect books and the remaining coyote, raven, and other animal-shaped ingredients jars to finish the move to the junk truck.

"What do you want me to do?" I ask, expecting her to assign me a shit job.

"Go help Fig pack up the mystical weapons."

"Where?" I'm quick to respond, thinking she's being nice for a change, and it might be a fun job.

"In the vault. Last door on the right, by the exit." Then she whistles and commands me like a dog, "Come on, boy. Let's go."

We proceed down the gray hallway with concrete block walls and a smooth cement floor. I glance over my shoulder at the laundry room entrance and the staircase that ascends to the lobby, remembering the earlier escapade with Chump and Javier. Cramps churn in my gut: part antidote, part worry about failure.

"Barry," Candy shouts, her voice echoing.

"What?" I turn to face the exit to the parking lot, the door held ajar by a nun. Candy's in front of it, looking at me over her shoulder.

"Hurry up." She nods toward the door beside her. "Vault's in there. Grab whatever you can carry and bring it to the old junky truck outside. I'll join you guys after dropping this off."

"Okay," I say, wondering why we're trusting our transport to a vehicle that sounds ready to breakdown at any moment, magic or no magic.

"Stop wasting time."

I slip into a small gym, mirrored on one wall and dimly lit. Mats cover most of the floor. In the far-right corner a punching bag hangs from the ceiling, and a few bashed up broom handles rest against the wall. This must be the sparing room Chump mentioned earlier, when they were scamming me into a trip to the pub.

Across from the entry, light glows around an open vault door with a combination lock and spin handle. I hear footsteps and hedge toward the gap.

"Hey, Fig, you in there?" I call out while pulling on the door handle. The hinges squeak.

No one answers.

The storage area, slightly larger than the apothecary, contains a few wooden boxes stored on shelves on the opposite wall. On the shelf beside me sits a mace and a crossbow. One more trip and this room will be vacant.

A long wood-carved case floats off the shelf and suspends mid-air. Have the bounty hunters arrived, cloaked?

My heart pounds as I reach for the crossbow. The hair trigger releases, and an arrow takes flight, hitting an invisible target below where the container's suspended.

A shriek resonates, and I'm taken aback.

Fig materializes with the arrow in her abdomen. She drops the box, her expression a mix of wonder and pain as she collapses.

The crossbow slips from my hand and goes off again, the shaft lodging in the floor beside my foot.

Shit. But my only thought is for Fig as I rush to her side, repeating her name. My first impulse is to remove the arrow, but when I touch it, she groans.

"Are you okay?" I stroke her arm.

She answers with a weep and a gurgle.

"I'm so sorry."

What to do?

Junk truck.

Candy enters and hollers, "What happened?"

My voice raises a few octaves as I spew what happened. "A container. It floated off the shelf. I thought we were under attack. The crossbow. Hair trigger. Went off."

"Why didn't you come find me before you picked up…" She points and asks, "Oh God, you shot that?"

"I'm so sorry." My gut churns with guilt. "She was invisible."

"Fig prefers 'they,' moron. They're a Qarinah. A succubus able to changes sexes at will, and they disappear when nervous."

"A succubus?" *In a hotel?* Seems the best place for their kind to live.

"That thing shoots infinite poison arrows." She squats, grasps the shaft, and pulls it out. "We've got to get them to Ulla and Inez."

Fig's breathing quickens when Candy lifts them like a baby.

"Use my shirt as a bandage." I motion to strip it off.

"No. Bleeding is the least of their worries. There's magic in the tip that closes the wound to keep the toxins inside the body," she says. "Grab that olive wood box and the crossbow. Follow me to the junk truck… and try not to shoot me."

I follow orders, and figure I deserve every insult she dishes out. Then, as I gather the weapons and turn off the light, a loud commotion sounds in the hallway.

"What was that?" I ask.

Candy shushes me and creeps into the gym. I rush to catch up, the box under one arm and the crossbow held in the other, aimed at the ceiling. A skak with teeth bared runs into the training area. Before I can take aim, the crumpled mummy leaps, latches onto my calf, and bites through my jeans and flesh. I shoot him through the ear with a poison arrow, but he's still holding on, as if frozen in place. So, I drop the box, pull him off me, and throw him against the punching bag. Just for fun, I shoot him again.

The pain in my leg drops me to my knees.

"Kissamyass," Candy whispers while examining my wound. "Get up."

"Can't…. hurts." Along with a groan and a few mumbled curse words, I prop myself up using the crossbow and manage to stand, but then realize I forget to pick up the other weapon. "Could you get that for me?"

Candy ignores me and puts Fig on the matted floor. Instead of lifting the olive wood box, she opens it and pulls out a sword that looks as if it would shatter when sliced through butter. "Where there's one of those freaks, there are bound to be more." She skulks toward the exit and peeks through the opening between the door and the jamb.

"Hey, I don't feel so good."

She tiptoes back to Fig and me with a wrinkled brow and a huff. "What now?"

"Head hurts, bad." I start to sway.

"Why haven't you healed yet?" She examines me, from top to bottom. "The sooner you guys get to the junk truck, the better, but there are half a dozen skaks standing near the laundry room. Probably jumped in through the dryer. So, here's what we're going to do. You carry Fig and the Sword of Sin outside."

"Sword of Sin?" I ask as we exchange weapons.

"Yeah, baby, this is it… and we can't risk losing it," she says. "If Azael is in the area, it'll weaken him, but it will also weaken Trisha and any other angels, so be careful."

My legs wobble as Candy helps me lift Fig over my shoulder. They grunt, and I pray for a miracle we can make it to the junk truck.

"Let's move." Candy tiptoes toward the exit, and I follow. "Don't look back, no matter what. Got it?"

"Yes." My senses key in on the sound of shuffling feet in the hallway.

"Tell Pete to leave without me."

"What? No."

"Don't worry about me. Get Fig to safety."

This time I nod.

Candy glances through the door crack before pushing me into the hallway. "Go. Hurry."

Careful not to slip into hyper-speed, I take off.

"Hey, assholes," she shouts.

I stop outside the basement exit and see why she said not to look back. The skaks have multiplied like rabbits, and Roy Morrow's towering over them in the center of the pack. While Candy shoots poison arrows at machine gun speed and plows through shriveled mummies, the caveman stands firm, waving his sword, stopping every airborne threat.

When Roy sees me, he growls and forces his way through the crowd. I lose sight of Candy as she falls through the laundry's doorway, covered in skaks.

Chapter 23

THE JUNK truck's right outside the basement door, where Candy said it would be. It's the size of a pickup with a bed full of wood scraps, pipes, and assorted building salvage. The smell of gasoline fills the surrounding air.

Beside the open tailgate, Pete snaps his attention to us. So does Sister Theresa's from where she's exiting between two sheets of plywood, slanted together to form a triangle.

"Go!" I approach them, juggling Fig and the Sword of Sin. "We've gotta go, now."

"What happened?" His arms reach out to meet us.

I wheeze and slow to a trudge. "Fig needs help. Shot with a poison arrow." I avoid telling him it's my fault.

"Where's Candy?" He takes the Sword of Sin and stares at the hotel entrance.

"Holding off Roy Morrow…" I set Fig on the tailgate and gasp for air. "…and skaks. Loads of skaks."

Pete holds the weapon up as if he's preparing to charge into battle.

"We've got to help her." The wide-eyed Sister Theresa calls into the black plywood gap, "Sisters!"

Two veiled nuns pop their heads out of the opening, both alert and ready for action.

"She said to leave her."

"Yes." Pete tweaks. "She's right. Bring Fig to Ulla and Inez. We're leaving."

"But Candy," Sister Theresa says as the other nuns pull Fig's limp body into the triangle gap that appears to be the entry into the junk truck.

A fierce pain stabs at the back of my head. My injured leg collapses. I grasp the tailgate to prevent a fall and tell Pete, "Skak bite."

"Get him inside." He seems in control of his demon, but for how long?

Sister Theresa jumps to the pavement. They push and tug, launching my dead weight onto the vehicle. Two nuns drag me toward the opening when a loud bang sounds.

The metal door into the hotel's basement thrusts open. Roy storms out and pauses near a trash dumpster. With his sword in hand, he swipes at the air and snarls, warning he's about to chop us into millions of pieces.

"Sisters, hurry." Sister Theresa climbs onto the truck bed and pushes my feet. I scream in agony. My head dizzies while everyone appears to be in fast forward.

They drag me inside, my body shivering from the cold aluminum-threaded floor. We proceed through a narrow hallway with walls composed of stacked containers, mainly wooden crates but some cardboard and metal boxes that disappear into a ceiling of white light that makes me squint. Each box bears a label drawn in a sort of hieroglyph, a language maybe only God can read.

As Pete joins us, still clutching the Sword of Sin, his cowboy boots ping across the floor. "Go! Drive!" he shouts. With no driver in sight, there's no telling who he's addressing or if this vehicle drives itself.

The truck jerks as if the gas pedal's being pushed to the metal. The momentum of the departure throws us off balance, and Pete and the nuns stumble. I fall backward and bang my head on the floor, causing my brain and leg to throb in unison.

"We're safe now," Pete says while looking down at me, lying flat on my back. "Once this truck takes off, it disappears, like Trisha mentioned earlier. It's here, but it's not here."

Sure, he says we're protected, but I still don't fully understand how this vehicle works. And all I can think about is Candy, left behind. What about her safety?

Pete points the Sword of Sin at my fleshy gash, exposed through the blood-stained rip in my jeans. A horrible cramp spreads through my body. I hold my knee and screech.

"Why is that not healing?" Pete sucks air through his teeth, then his eyes pop. "Shit, it's the Sword of Sin."

"Huh?" I say with a long groan.

"Because you're half angel, it must be weakening you." He takes off down the hallway and hollers, "Take Barry to Ulla and Inez. I need to find an olive wood box."

The nuns hover and arrange my arms over my chest before reaching around my back and thighs to form a hammock. As I'm lifted off the ground, my neck collapses from a migrating paralysis. The thought of the Sword of Sin rendering me helpless, as it does to angels, is terrifying. What other defense do I have against my father?

The ladies carry me through a maze of containers, packed together like a brick wall on each side. Every few seconds, the hieroglyphic labels blur and change in design.

We stop and Sister Theresa says, "The labyrinth shifted again. Any ideas how we find Ulla and Inez?"

"What happened?" I slur.

A nun with bright blue eyes says, "This vehicle constantly shifts to better hide the contents. We've hit a wall that wasn't here five minutes ago."

"Turn left," another nun says. "Ulla mentioned to always turn left if we get lost."

As we press on, I hope this search doesn't take days. Who knows the actual size of this place? And I'm getting that the surrounding relics want to stay hidden.

Three turns later, Ulla's in my face. "Poor boy. What happened?"

Inez grumbles and pulls my nose. "More trouble with you."

Ulla says, "Put him on the sarcophagus."

I swallow hard and struggle to speak through tingly lips. "I'm not dead."

They set me on the solid surface. I catch sight of Fig on the other side of the room, on the familiar metal exam table. What appears to be a mud pack covers the puncture on their stomach. I shiver from the state of Fig and the cold rock.

While Sister Theresa describes my injury, I scan the compact space, walled off by more crates. Potion jars, emitting the usual apothecary smells, and old books rest on solitary boxes and the floor.

A nun spreads a space blanket over me. "This will warm you."

"Thank you."

Sister Theresa grasps my hand and leans in close. "You'll be fine."

"How's Fig?" I ask.

Everyone freezes. No one answers. Oh, God, what did I do to them?

"Let's take a look at that bite," Ulla says, followed by the sound of my jeans ripping.

"Black veins… spreading," Inez observes and snaps her fingers. "Bring catfish jar."

"Could the Sword of Sin be draining him?" Sister Theresa asks. "Barry had it in his hand when he exited the hotel with Fig. His pain intensified as Pete held the tip near the wound."

Inez nods. "But we must also rule out bite."

This place is crazy: so many hovering faces, the labels on the containers changing, and the potion odors. *Don't puke. Don't puke.* I scream as an extra sharp pain shoots from my calf to my thigh. My head spins and I dry heave.

"No vomiting." Inez slaps my forehead. "Keep antidote in stomach."

"Sorry, dear," Ulla says. "We're applying a salve that will hurt more as the potion soaks in. Must be done to verify the source of what's weakening you."

Pete enters and peers down at me. "I found an olive wood container for the Sword of Sin. Barry should start feeling better. I'm just worried the new box might shift with the other boxes, and we'll lose it."

"If you need it, God will keep it fixed," Inez says. "He will deliver the sword back to us."

"You sure?" Without pause, he adds, "How are you, Barry?"

"Pains worse. Hurts bad." I hold my breath and clench my jaw.

"Oh, my." Ulla turns to her other half. "Should we put him under?"

"Do it," Pete says. "If he's asleep, he can't cause trouble."

Sister Theresa adds, "And maybe he won't vomit while asleep."

"Don't I get a vote?" I lift my hands as the two-headed lady hovers near the side of my face holding a wiggly worm. It crawls into my ear, and I yawn. "What is with your creepy crawlies? What'd you put…?"

"Snooze larva."

"Get it out!"

Inez wiggles her finger in my ear canal. "Pete says you sleep, I make you sleep."

"No," I whisper and fight to keep my eyes open, but I lose and fade into darkness.

Chapter 24

I WAKE UP surrounded by rock and the sound of a crinkly space blanket. While sitting up on an uncomfortable cot, my head pulses near my temples and hair raises on my arms from the damp chill in the air. At least the pain in my leg is gone.

Unless it was amputated? I jerk, wiggle my toes, and pat my calf. *Thank God. Still there.* Now is not the time to regrow another limb.

The ceiling is low and so is the narrow entryway near the end of the cot. This place must be a cavity in Trisha's cave. Guess we made it, but is everyone safe? Or just those who were in the junk truck. And how long have I been unconscious?

Water. I smack dry lips.

When my eyes adjust to the candlelit cavern, it's obvious this room was turned into an apothecary. Makes sense they'd leave me here along with the nearby body atop the familiar metal exam table. With some sort of webbing covering every part of the motionless figure, it's difficult to discern who it is. Did the two-headed lady find a cure for Fig?

"Bear. You're finally awake."

My attention snaps toward Nina's sweet and choppy voice in the glowing doorway, but my smile drops as I get a good look at her. "What the fuck?" I jump up, the space blanket sliding to the floor. "You're a white warrior!"

Nina's naked and pale. Folded wings rise behind her shoulders. Seeing her sexless with claw-like fingers and talons for feet is even more revolting.

"What's the matter?" She tilts her head, and her eyes glow orange.

Is she really questioning my protest? "You're a white warrior," I repeat.

"It's okay." She flutters her wings. "Flying is fun."

"Dammit, Nina, it's not okay." I frown, stumble a few steps, then grasp her arm, ready to drag her with me to confront Trisha.

"Not Nina. Nita now."

I release her and pause. "Nita?"

"Yes," she says, all cheery. "When we were turned, Gita and Nina became one. We became me. Nita."

Heat flows over my cheeks. Why would Trisha do this? Why would she risk Nina's identity as a human or as a Daughter of Light? Sure, I wanted Nina protected from Azael, but why turn her into a white warrior?

"Bear? You alright?" Nita stares up at me wide-eyed and biting her lip.

With bared teeth, I growl, then rush from the room on unsteady legs, whacking my head on the low opening. "Trisha! Where the hell are you? What did you do?"

Chapter 25

ALL EYES are on me as I limp into a cavern that's slightly larger than a high school gymnasium. Near the center of the room, Pete, Candy, and Sister Theresa stand beside a granite slab table. The tall, jagged ceiling echoes my objection as I shout, "What the hell! Why is Nina a white warrior?"

On the other side of the cave, a half dozen nuns pause their sparring weapons mid-swipe and turn to stare.

"Barry." Pete smiles and rolls up a sleeve on his white shirt. As he approaches, his cowboy boots clunk on the rock floor. "You're awake. How's the leg?"

"Don't change the subject." Rapid breaths fill my lungs with damp air. "What about Nina? I mean Nita. Or whatever the hell her name is now."

"I understand your concern." Pete maintains a safe distance as he swoops an inviting hand toward their meeting place. "Please, join us. I'll explain."

I hesitate. "Where's Trisha?"

"Here we go again." Candy, dressed in tight-fitted camouflage, steps forward with her fists clenched at her side. A long, unwrapped licorice rope hangs beside her left thigh and grazes spit-shined combat boots. For once, she's wearing appropriate footwear. "After everything you've put us through, all you care about is that… that… pain in everyone's ass."

"Sorry." Relieved she's alive, I shift focus and ask, "It's good to see you. How'd you get away? Are you okay?"

"Me kicking skak butt is the least of our worries." She bites one end of the wrapper off the licorice and spits it at my lame leg. "Have you forgotten Margery kidnapped Javier? Any consideration for the twenty-four hours we've lost while you played sleeping beauty? Or that Fig is dead, also because of you?"

Fig… dead? A day lost? My mouth drops. No wonder she thinks I'm an asshole.

"I really am sorry." I hang my head for two seconds before turning to Pete. "Wait a minute. I slept for a full day. Why? I mean, how could the Sword of Sin on top of a skak bite weaken me that badly?" Trying to lighten the moment, I chuckle and joke, "I'm *no* angel."

"No… you're *not*." Candy peels plastic from the red rope; her insult and the crinkling wrapper grate on my nerves.

"If you two are done…" Pete leans over the table and shakes his head. When he turns to me, I move in closer and notice his violet eyes emit a brighter, pulsing color, like Nina's do when her demon takes control. "You are Nephilim. You are half angel."

"I know. I was just—"

Pete snorts… then hiccups… then clears his throat. "Respect a blade crafted from parts Spear of Destiny, part spike that held Jesus on the cross. It's a dangerous combo for any angel, light or dark, and now we can add Nephilim to the list."

Sister Theresa adds. "Took eight hours alone for Ulla and Inez to stabilize you."

"And knowing how it weakens you…" Candy casually returns to the table, the camouflage pattern on her pants swaying with her hips. She munches licorice and adds, "… all we have to do is open that Sword of Sin box to knock you on your ass."

"Hilarious." Continuing to gaze at her rear end, my stomach growls. An expected response after a two-day slumber, but my usual desire for a bowl of fruity cereal has been replaced with a strange and repulsive urge. I hold my gut. This can't be right. Never in a million years would I want to eat human flesh, let alone indulge in a sudden craving to bite Candy's rump roast.

"Not funny," Pete says. "We need Barry healthy and strong, and the way God designed him to wipe Azael's existence."

"The way God designed me? What exactly does that mean?"

They look at each other, eyes wide, an awkward silence lingering. Seems they've already decided my fate, taking out a fallen angel.

Candy jumps in. "Should someone check on Nassar?"

"C'mon. Don't change the subject. You can't keep me in the dark forever." But even I lose focus when a cramp stabs at my stomach. My attention shifts to Candy' bulging backside again. Despite it being composed of human flesh and melted demon essence, it's enticing… tempting. Saliva builds in my mouth.

This has to be skak absorption from the bite. I wipe my lips, concentrate on a dark water spot on the table, and tell myself, *Fight it.*

"Barry?" Pete narrows in on me.

Still staring, I listen to my gut plead for flesh and fan the sweat building on my brow. My tongue ties as I say, "What's going on? Nothing makes sense. What are you hiding?"

"Barry!" Pete snaps his fingers.

I turn to him. "We got any fruit flavored cereal?" With any luck, my all-time favorite food will suppress these cannibalistic cravings. Or buy me some time while I figure a way to stifle these skak tendencies.

Candy sighs. "I'll get it."

"Extra-large bowl, please," I call out, careful to stare at the ceiling instead of her butt as she shuffles toward the sparring nuns. I'm glad she's the one leaving the room to fetch my cereal.

"Barry, you're pale," Sister Theresa says. "Maybe you should sit down. Have some water. You could be dehydrated." She pours me a glass.

"Thanks, but I'm fine." Although I drink it anyway to help suppress the hunger. "Where *is* Nassar?"

"Well…" Pete drills an index finger on the table and avoids eye contact.

"Well, what?" I ask.

In a whiny voice, Pete blurts out, "Gita extracted the Qarinah from Fig's body and put it in Nassar." He jerks erect, smooths back strands of black hair, and glares with a contorted guise of, 'call me Jack Nickolas in *The Shining*.' "Nina's demon conducted the transfer against Nassar's will."

"Was that Boss talking?" I ask Sister Theresa.

"Hey, asshole, I can speak for myself," Boss says, but I ignore him.

The Reverend Mother nods and explains, "It's why Trisha turned Nina and Gita into a white warrior. She was hoping to gain control over the two, but they ended up merging into Nita, a much worse version. Not even Trisha expected the merger to go that bad."

I drop into a nearby chair, my arms limp at my sides. A million questions flood my brain, and I start by asking, "So, Fig's dead, and that's Nassar in the cavern where I woke up?"

Again, she nods, then takes a seat, folding her hands over her lap. "When a Qarinah enters a new body, it requires a transition period, like a butterfly. Nassar's cocooned in the apothecary, transitioning into a gender-shifter. The process can take up to a week."

"Please tell me he's not suffering."

"Physically, there's no pain." Sister Theresa says.

"That's a good thing, right?"

"Didn't you hear Boss say 'against Nassar's will'?" Candy says while returning with my bowl of fruity cereal. Her shaky hands spill milk that splatters on the floor. "He wanted to remain a man, but when he wakes up, he could have a pussy."

"But Nassar dresses—"

Pete and Sister Theresa clear their throats.

"Aren't you young enough to understand gender and sexual orientation?" Candy drops the cereal in front of me, milk splashing everywhere, the spoon jumping from the bowl. "He may dress feminine, but he's a gay man. He enjoys having a cock, and he enjoys sucking—"

"Candy!" Pete goes into another twitching fit.

"Oh, get over it," she says. "How would any of you feel if, in an instant, the demon that possesses you decided a situation required a vagina?"

"Sorry. You're right. I do understand the whole gender thing, but why would Gita make such a decision for Nassar?" I shovel a spoonful of cereal into my mouth.

"Ulla and Inez couldn't save Fig's body," Sister Theresa says. "As a Qarinah separates, its only option is to enter a new host within six hours. Otherwise, thousands of years of its memories and knowledge are wiped out after its essence is returned to the demon pool. But taking on a Qarinah means you lose all control over your body, and none of us are willing to take on that ability. We were prepared to let the demon return to Hell."

"Gita kept insisting Nassar become the new host," Pete says. "Despite him insisting the idea repulsed him, Gita transferred the Qarinah into Nassar. We're not sure when and how, but it happened while we were trying to move from the junk truck to the cave."

"Lucky for your girlfriend I wasn't here yet, because I would have ripped her head off." Candy wipes an eye.

"Sorry, so sorry that happened." I back away from the cereal, overcome by the memory of Margery doing the same to Nina a few days ago, possessing her with Gita. Why it seems so crazy she would let Gita do the same to someone else.

"What's done is done," Pete says. "Trisha had no choice but to turn her into a white warrior, so it's senseless to discuss this any further."

I nod, but there's no way I'll accept what Trisha's done to her. Instead, I concentrate on the terrible things that have happened to Fig and Nassar. And when he wakes up, he'll blame it all on me.

Candy reaches over the table for another licorice rope, and I concede that the fruity flavor isn't suppressing my appetite for flesh. My gut gurgles and churns at a level that causes everyone to turns to me. Then my jaw seems to have a mind of its own, opening against my will.

Why crave… Candy? Although I could devour everyone at the table, serving myself a three-course meal. And my grumbling gut wouldn't refuse nun cobbler for dessert.

"Hey!" Candy points at me. "The skaks in the laundry room had that look of hunger on their faces. Can't believe I missed it."

I bare my teeth and survey her butt.

"Barry!" Pete yells. "What are you doing?"

But there's no stopping me. I take off toward Candy, slide in on my knees, and bite the side of her ass.

Chapter 26

CANDY GRABS me around the head, flips me off my feet, and snaps my spine. Face planted on the cold rock floor, my cheek rests in a puddle of cave drippings. After a few seconds of rapid blinking, I realize I'm paralyzed.

"You bwoke my neck," I lisp with a tongue half-bitten through. Of all the dumb things I've done the last few weeks, this tops them all. Well, except for signing my life over to Satan.

She stands over me. "Not very smart, trying to make a meal of a psychic."

"Some psychic. Took you forever to figure it out."

She grinds the soul of her boot into my ear. "I can still shove the Sword of Sin up your ass."

"Uncle! Uncle!" I then realize my tongue has fused, and I can wiggle my fingers and toes. Good to know my rapid healing has been restored.

She lifts me off the ground by the back of my jeans and drags me to an antique metal chair that belongs in a World War II bunker. As she slams me into the vinyl seat, it tilts and falls backward. My head crashes against the floor and explodes with pain.

"C'mon." Coppery spit trickles into my throat, making me choke.

She walks toward the sparring nuns to collect a chain, then uses it to pull me upright and tie me into the chair.

"Seriously? Is this necessary?"

"My ass says it is." She moves in close and slaps my cheek. "Such an idiot."

"I'm tired of everyone calling me stupid." Bright red spit particles land on her face.

Candy stands erect, her lips puckered, and wipes her eyes with the backs of her hand.

"You really think I'd bite *your* ass on purpose." Overcome with disgust for having cannibalistic tendencies, I shiver. "The skak bite. I absorbed their taste for… flesh."

"Barry, Barry, Barry," Pete says, his expression conveying his usual disappointment. "Why didn't you mention this as soon as you figured it out?"

"So selfish." With her Superman strength, she lifts my chair from behind and shoves me hard against the edge of the table. I choke. A dull pain spreads from my sternum. "Try to bite me again, and you're dead."

"Enough!" Pete turns toward Sister Theresa. "Please go tell Ulla and Inez about Barry's hunger. I'm sure they can whip up something that will stifle his cravings."

Candy adds, "Suggest they season it with extra hot peppers—"

"Stop the bickering!" Pete says.

While Sister Theresa leaves, Pete and Candy pace on opposite sides of the table.

Afraid she's dreaming up new and improved forms of punishment, I hit her with a distraction. "So… how'd you escape the hotel?

Candy freezes, then pivots on one heel to face me. "For one thing, Roy Morrow's no longer a threat."

"Did you chop off his head?"

"Better." She steps closer and rubs her ass. "Crows flew in carrying a few bounty hunters. They were pissed that *you* got away but were glad I'd cleared most of the skaks. Plus, they were quick to settle for Roy instead. He has an active Warrant for Damnation that's almost as valuable as yours."

"What did he do to land on Satan's Most Wanted List?"

Pete jumps in. "Appears he's working for Margery and Azael."

"No shit." I laugh. "That guy is freakin' crazy."

Our attention turns to the two-headed lady, waddling around a corner near the sparing nuns. She carries a tray, and Ulla's head rests on the shoulder on her side with eyes closed as if she's snoozing. Or did I somehow kill her too?

"Is Ulla okay?" I ask Pete, hoping to avoid a lecture from Inez.

Doesn't stop her from answering. "You cause too much trouble. We take turns, napping."

Inez drops the tray on the table. An empty shot glass hops and black liquid splashes out of the other. I try to stay focused on Candy's story as my mouth goes dry, anticipating the rancid flavor of the next brew I'll have to drink.

Candy continues her story. "Because I helped the bounty hunters capture Roy and decapitate the rest of the skaks, Satan suspended your warrant for seventy-two hours. Unfortunately, you slept through twenty-four of them."

"My warrant's a joke. Satan should want me free to eliminate his brother… his competition."

Inez smacks the back of my head and holds the empty shot glass up to my mouth. "Spit."

With a mouth still dry, I hack and cough, and work up a ball of saliva. Everyone but Inez cringes.

Candy stiffens. "Stupid and gross."

This time, I ignore the insult, more so because Inez has the full shot glass up to my lips. I gulp the black solution like a shot of Jagermeister, but surprisingly there's no odor or flavor. "Wow, that was easy."

"Yes, part one is easy," Inez says. "This potion starts process. We use saliva for second potion. Will return in an hour with next step. Uses the volcanic magic, so it could burn."

I sigh as Ulla and Inez waddle toward the cavern where I woke up. Of course, Candy laughs, but if she's happy, I'm at least safe from her torture.

"So," I say, "I have forty-eight hours to destroy my dad, without the CEO of Hell getting in my business?"

"Yes," Pete says.

"Still don't understand why Satan's not grateful I exist."

"He's more concerned that God will send you after him once you've erased Azael," Pete says.

I nod and consider that the logic may make sense to the leader of Hell, but my past trip to the damned refugee camp was enough of an incentive to avoid him and that realm for an eternity.

"Why don't you just tell me where to find Azael?" I say. "I'll give him a big reuniting bear hug and—"

"If only it were that simple," Pete says.

"And you were that brave," Candy adds.

"Ha, ha." My body stiffens against the chain. "At this point, I don't care what happens to me."

Trisha's Stiletto heels click on the rock floor, interrupting our discussion. "There are way too many risks for you to attempt it alone. Assuming you're successful with your hug, absorbing Azael could corrupt you."

"Yeah." Candy smirks. "You couldn't even control yourself after one skak bite."

Great. Now that Trisha's returned, the two can tag team me.

I lower my head. "I told you, I didn't want to bite your ass."

Chump arrives with an ax bouncing off his shoulder. He laughs and holds his stomach. "Whose ass did you bite?"

"Never mind," I say.

"You guys are being unfair," Chump says. "Barry had my back at the Earthbound Spirit's Pub. Count me first in line to go into battle with him."

"Wow." Candy ticks a mark in the air. "Give Barry a point for one good deed out of how many fuck ups?"

"Stop being such a bitch." Chump drops his ax on the table with a loud clang, then sits in Sister Theresa's place.

"Please. Barry is far from a joke." Pete exhales and adjusts his shoulders as if he's fighting a twitch. Then he turns up an evil grin, and I guess that Boss adds, "He has the whole Catholic Church shitting their pants."

This could turn catastrophic. They feared witches too. Woman after suspicious woman, dunked in water and burned at the stake. What will they do to keep me in line? So, I have to ask, "Do I at least get a say on how we take out Azael?"

Simultaneously, everyone says, "No." Their voices echo against the cave wall.

Trisha closes in on Pete, bringing with her the usual welcoming rose fragrance. "The plan's been granted by God, and the Vatican has handed the details down to us."

"So, what you're saying is… *He*, who gave us humans free will, has the last word on how I take out *His* angel?"

They respond with frowns and sighs and crossed arms and tapping feet.

"Does their, or at least His grand scheme include me absorbing my father's abilities?"

"Yes," Pete says. "They acknowledge your power to rob others of their… faculties. The problem is what might happen before, during, and after your confrontation with Azael. Try to understand that we are preparing for the worst possible outcome."

"You guys have to trust me." I laugh, realizing how foolish I sound.

"Barry," Trisha says, "you're able to move as fast as lightning, shoot Margery's cigarettes from your palms, and breathe fire."

"Don't forget he's a freakin' cannibal." Candy looks over her shoulder at her butt.

Do they believe I'm the first step toward the end of the world? "Why is everyone treating me as if I'm more dangerous than Azael?"

"Because you are." Trisha taps a fingernail against her crossed arm. "For one thing, once you exhibit Azael's powers, Satan will want to get his hands on you even more. Word will spread that you can steal powers, and every underworld being out there will want you dead. That's just the beginning of what could happen to you, which is why we are here to help you and keep you safe, even though it sounds like we're against you."

I slump, and the chain tightens around my stomach. Her frightening scenarios conveniently left out *their* plan for me once I've absorbed a fallen angel. Will I take a turn sitting in an eternal prison? Will God turn me against another fallen angel? The scenarios are endless, but it's naïve to believe they'd let me go free. All I can do is live in the now.

"What do you want me to do?"

They look at each other.

Trisha scratches the tip of her nose.

"Well," Pete says, "you won't like this, but the plan starts with Nita being delivered to Azael."

My heart skips a beat. "No… fucking… way."

Chapter 27

I CALL TOWARD the apothecary, "Nina! Nita, get out here!"

"She's already agreed to distract Azael," Trisha says, "although trusting her is still up for debate. Anyway, it's the best way to camouflage your approach."

"Let me hear it from Nina." I snap back.

"Nita," Candy corrects, her grin telling she revels in every opportunity to make me feel stupid.

"Nina. Gita. Nita," I struggle to escape my restraints. "She's too vulnerable to throw into the middle of Margery's camp."

"Vulnerable? Ha!" Candy gets in my face. "She cut off the head of a courier she possessed and sunk the boarding house. Yesterday, she forced Fig's demon to take over Nassar's body."

"That was all Gita. Nina is harmless." I bounce in the chair some more, frustrated my argument is weak. "You should have given her that demon suppressant."

"Won't stop her from wanting to spread her legs for your father," Candy says.

"Barry, please, we tried what we could," Trisha says. "If Gita had killed anyone—"

"Fine. I get it. She's got her own agenda."

A white-as-a-ghost Nita jogs out of the apothecary, her talons click clacking against the floor. She slides to a stop beside my chair. "Bear, you want me to untie you?"

"Sure."

"No!" Trisha hollers. "Hold still."

Nita seems to snap to attention, her orange eyes wide.

"She called me Bear, Nina's nickname for me. She's gotta be in there."

Trisha gets in my face. "All manipulation. A deadly combo of demon and Daughter of Light. I'm the only one who can control her now."

"Why'd you have to do it? Why'd you turn her into a white warrior?"

"You wanted her kept away from your father," Trisha says. "Besides, with her being sexless, you got what you wanted. Azael can't impregnate her.

I hang my head and close my eyes, searching for something to say that might change their minds about using Nita. Nothing comes to mind that I haven't already said.

"Bear, don't worry about me. I want to help. God created me for this."

"See," Candy says. "And this is probably the only way we can work with Gita."

"It's okay. You won't fail." Nita wiggles her talons. "And I'll get my chance to claw out Margery's eyes."

I grit my teeth and struggle against the chains. Seems all that matters is Nita's compliance. They're crazy if they think I'll give up on her.

"If we're done with the Nita debate, is anyone interested in what we found at the sand dunes?" Trisha asks.

"Pretty ugly out there," Chump says with a wide toothy grin. "Where's the whiskey?"

"No more liquor." Pete calls across the room, "Sisters, gather around. Everyone needs to take part in this discussion."

Trisha starts while they gather. "Margery's dug up at least a hundred skak mummies, and there are still more in the ground. She's also moved her hellhounds and Minotaurs to the upper region of the sand dunes. It's a full and functioning encampment, and the area's well-guarded.

"Except for an opening we found that's a perfect place for Barry to sneak up on Azael," Chump adds.

"Great news." Pete faces the nuns. "Sisters, we need you all to pair up and surround Margery's camp. Candy and I will join you."

"Okay," I say with a frown, "you found a way in, but how do you intend to bring me to my father?"

"That's where Nita comes in," Trisha says. "Two of my white warriors will deliver her as bait to get Azael out of the trees he's been hanging out in."

"Wait, your white warriors are dead," I say to Trisha."

"I have three warriors who weren't solidified in the hellhole. Milar and Jill are still out watching the camp. When we get there, they'll fly with Nita into a clearing, as if they're defecting." She adds, "After Azael lands to meet Nita, you'll sneak in and—"

"What if he doesn't land?" I ask, thinking they're too confident in their Vatican approved plan.

The room goes silent.

Trisha lifts an eyebrow and bites down on her lower lip. "Azael *will* land when he sees Nita."

I lean in. "How can you be so sure he'll desire a sexless Daughter of Light?"

Pete blocks my line of questioning. "Barry, you'll be with Trisha, Chump, and Gorsky."

"Gorsky?" I ask.

Trisha turns to me. "The third and my most trusted warrior."

"The plan," Pete says, "is for Trisha and Gorsky to help you attach to Azael, and start the absorption process. If something appears to go wrong, or there's a perceived threat to humanity, Chump will remove the Sword of Sin from the box and—"

"He'll what?" I interrupt, eyes wide and voice raised.

The room goes silent again.

Chump looks at Trisha with a disagreeable scowl, then he pounds his knuckles against his chest. "Dismembering mummies and demons should be my job. But they want me to chop off your head if the shit hits the fan."

"Chump, we've been over this," Pete says. "The nuns are trained to have our backs. You're the best choice to wield the Sword of Sin and weaken Azael if things get out of hand."

"And weaken me," I mumble.

Heads turn to me, and Candy's quick to say, "Yes."

"Barry!" Trisha pops a hip. "We've been going over the details countless times while you've been sleeping. It *will* work. It has to. There is no approved Plan B, and we don't have time to create one."

"Fine. I'll go along with *your* plan." I hop in the chair, stare down at the chain, and grit my teeth. "Not that I have a choice." After all, God has never let my kind live, and by the look on Candy's face, she's ready to open the Sword of Sin box and take me out before we even reach the sand dunes.

Ulla and Inez return, both awake this time, a large cup with steam rising off it in one hand.

Candy turns toward them. "Thank God. I hope that's the antidote."

"We can only hope," Ulla says in her sweet voice.

"What do you mean?" Candy asks.

As I'm handed the cup, Ulla explains, "This is a new brew to counteract effects from a new type of being… which was imposed on Barry, a rare being. And with Father Timothy dead, the Vatican is not cooperative in allowing us to access the volcanic magic archive."

Inez adds, "Fifty fifty chances of success."

Candy turns to Pete. "With odds like that, maybe I should wield the Sword of Sin. I mean, I'm ready, willing, and able to take off his—"

"Shut up and untie me, so I can save myself from biting your ass again."

Chapter 28

A N HOUR later, *their* plan is in motion. Under the glow of the full moon, Trisha leads the way through sparse pine trees in a wooded area west of the Great Sand Dunes. The breeze has a bite, as it usually does on a June night in the Colorado mountains. I rub my arms and wish a windbreaker covered them, but there's no level of coverage that could comfort my shaky nerves.

Loose and unstable sand that's been blowing around this area for four-hundred thousand years slips under my skater shoes. I'm thrown off balance and lean backward, caught by something sharp. Looking over my shoulder, it's the box containing the Sword of Sin, towed under Chump's left arm, that broke my fall. Saved by the very weapon meant to kill me if I don't do what I'm told.

I mouth to Chump, "Sorry."

Gorsky lifts the crossbow that killed Fig and aims it at my heart, but Chump lowers the weapon and acknowledges me with a nod. He then whispers something to the jerky white warrior who seems set on offing me before I have a chance to absorb the father I've never known.

This is turning into a dead man walking scenario. I should run. Take off at supersonic speed. Leave them in the lurch. But they'd find me. Hunt me down like they have every other Nephilim and shove the Sword of Sin up my ass like Candy continues to promise.

Trisha stops, motions us closer, and whispers, "Clearing's twenty yards ahead. Hear the skak chatter and clinking shovels?"

My stomach drops, and I'm frozen as I listen. When Chump and

Gorsky confirm, I wonder if they're also terrified, although nothing seems to intimidate Chump.

"They're on the other side of the clearing, digging up more of their kind." Trisha points between two large and shadowy pine trees with branches that start four feet above the ground. "Through there." She proceeds and we follow.

While staring into the open space the size of a football field, there's no telling how much farther Margery's demonic crew extends into the trees. And if they know we're here, they could be closing in on our current location. My shoulders tighten, respecting that the slightest sound could alert a hellhound. I scan for anything that glows orange or growls in the distance. Clear… so far. Pete's assurance that a single poison arrow from the crossbow Gorsky carries will drop any creature in its track is no comfort. Especially since he admitted he's no sharpshooter.

Someone steps on a stick, and it snaps. Trisha shushes us again, then she whispers in my ear, "Is the human appetite suppressant working?"

I nod, even though my gut growls for a nun burger. Still, it's easier to ignore the temptation than it was earlier.

"Are you sure?" She purses her lips.

"You want to control me? Turn me into a white warrior," I say, holding out hope she'll grant me the ability to fly to my father and give him a power sucking bear hug.

"No deviating," Trisha says. "I'll carry you to Azael."

I clench my fists, resentment building against the Catholic Church's prescribed plan. They might be against any potential Plan B, but I'm prepared to steal whatever faculties I need to protect myself and get the job done.

Chump reaches into one of his many pockets and pulls out a switchblade. "At least let him have this."

Trisha snatches it away. "Barry's absorption abilities are weapon enough."

"Bullshit. He won't hurt us." Chump takes it back and holds the knife out to me.

I throw up my hands.

"Fine," she says.

I mouth a thank you and tightly grip the handle.

To the right of the entrance into the clearing, we gather behind a bunch of trees. Trisha points skyward. "Shit's about to go down."

Three winged beings circle the area like giant bats. My heart races at the sight of Nita's long white hair flapping in the wind alongside Jill and Milar. Their white skin sparkles in the moonlight and wings whoosh as they descend and land center field.

They appear miniature when an airborne being descends and casts a vast shadow over our decoys and the sandy expanse. A bronze glow radiates off the creature's skin. It's Azael. Has to be. And he's three times the height of a man. Nita and the warriors peer into the sky, huddling together while the fallen angel swoops in to inspect the invaders and recedes to re-circle.

My body stiffens as I mull over being here, finally here, and realize I'll never be ready to confront my father the way they expect. Hell, I've never even met the guy, and he's never done anything to me on purpose. While I once thought he had abandoned me, turns out he's been imprisoned in these mountains. And according to Margery, he wants to give me everything, like any father would try to do. Still, I wonder, does he hope to atone for his absence or use me for his own gain?

"Why isn't he taking the bait?" I ask Trisha, worried that Azael appears hesitant to land. Does he know I'm here?

She shrugs. "No interest in a sexless white warrior? Maybe I should have returned her to human form."

Margery and a Minotaur, probably Bruno, dash in to meet Nita and the other white warriors. Even after the demon bitch makes her entrance, Azael still doesn't land. Instead, he continues to fly down to sniff Nita.

"Think he knows we're here?" Chump says in a low tone.

"If he does, we can't just stand here." I rock in place, and sand shifts under my feet, a warning there will be no speedy exit from this suicide mission.

"If they know we're here," Chump says, "their army of evil is already moving in."

"Ma-ma-maybe," Trisha stutters, "maybe we should make our way to Azael's tree."

"Maybe?" I say.

"I can't lose my wings again." She bites at the nail on her index finger.

"You'll lose 'em if we stand around doing nothing," I say, sure she's losing her nerve.

"Agreed." Chump says. "Even if we reach Azael's favorite tree, doesn't mean he'd be in it."

She points at the procession in the open space. "Look."

Sparks flicker from Margery's bobbing head as she shouts muffled curses and slaps Milar or Jill. Then Azael dives in and land beside Nita. His hands, the breadth of hubcaps, claw through the air, threatening the decoys.

I motion to run in but feel a tug on the back of my shirt.

"Not yet." Trisha says in a growl.

"What are we waiting for?" I glare at her. "*Your* plan is to rush him."

The fallen angel picks up a white warrior, bites off its head, and throws his body to the ground. Just like that, one of ours is down on his naked white stomach, his wings twitching. When Azael spits the warrior's head at Nita's feet, her lengthy scream floods the night.

Screw their plan.

"Nina!" I call out, only able to see her true self before I ruined her life. I sprint into the clearing, my skater shoes struggling against the loose sand.

"Barry, wait!" Chump follows, the Sword of Sin rattling in its box from behind, making me question if he's coming to stop me or help me.

All eyes are on me, but mine settle on Margery, growing and contorting into her reptilian demon form. She scoops up Nita and darts the direction where she had entered, her hair spewing sparks like a cluster of roman candles. At the same time, Azael imposes the same decapitation treatment on the other white warrior, discernable as Jill. While the evil bastard smacks his lips and savors the skull, the two warriors lie headless at his feet.

I stop short, my nervous thoughts chanting, *What am I doing? What am I doing?*

My father turns to meet Chump and me, his legs spread and palms together at his chest. Fat chance he's praying to God.

"Chump!" Trisha's in the air, circling us. "Use the sword!"

"No!" I call skyward. Why would she want to weaken me? I'm following the plan. Is her confidence in me that low? Or was this their play all along: destroy a fallen angel and a Nephilim, all at once?

"Fuck her," Chump says, now at my side, both of us paused twenty feet from my gigantic father. He places the Sword of Sin on the sandy surface, careful the container stays closed, then he swings his ax. "We can do this. Let's rush him. I'll chop him down like a tree. You jump him. Suck him dry of power."

At least I have one ally. But he has more faith in me than I have in myself.

Azael holds his position and claps; the thunderous sound nearly pops my eardrums. I poke at my ears.

Chump cries out in pain and drops to his knees, clutching his temples. His face contorts as he shouts something suppressed by my loss of hearing. When he yells a second time and points at Azael, I get the meaning. But I'm frozen with indecision: rush the fallen angel and be next to lose my head or open the sword box and sacrifice my strength.

In my hesitation, my father claps again. Chump's head separates from his neck and launches skyward, turning his body into a gushing fountain of blood. I track his head, soaring like a fly ball, as it descends to Earth. I catch him, face resting on my palms, the back of his skull split open, sticky brain matter exposed. Chump's fate is terrorizing, heartbreaking… and appetizing.

Shit! Ulla and Inez's human appetite suppressant has failed me at the worst time.

Don't do it. Don't eat it. But the impulse is too great. I lick my lips, crack open Chump's skull with shaky thumbs, and tear my teeth into his brain.

Chapter 29

A DULL PAIN hits the back of my head and halts my feast.

"Drop it!" Trisha punches my shoulder.

While staring into Chump's empty cranium, juice tickling my chin, the harsh reality sinks in. I've eaten his brain in record time. I release the skull to the sandy ground. My body quivers, wrestling with an urge to lick my fingers. Instead, I spit and nervously brush scalp and orange hair off my shirt.

"Hello... Son." Azael's deep laugh penetrates like thunder. "Did you bring my favorite little angel as a peace offering? She'll make a fine footstool or reading lamp."

"Fuck you," Trisha wags her fist, but shivers as if she's scared.

"I'll be the one *fucking...* you up, first taking pleasure in ripping off your wings again. Then I'll devour your light source whole." Azael sticks out a snake-like tongue that slurps and flits to tease her. "Bet you taste... *yummy.*"

Trisha flutters in place, then she jerks to the right and chases a Minotaur sneaking away with the wooden box containing the Sword of Sin. A flyaway feather attaches to my sticky hands. I try to shake it off but wipe it onto my shirt instead.

I'm left alone to face my monster of a father.

Azael holds his stomach and laughs. "Stupid angel apprentice. So gullible."

This is too easy for him. I should have done this by myself to begin with, like I told Pete.

"Go. Follow your sister." Azael leans forward and points toward where Margery took Nita. "Learn your place."

I stand by, remembering that God wants me to destroy this asshole. But I'm hesitant to move, fighting his dark pulsing gaze, a thing he handed down to Margery. What might this evil bastard force me to do if I don't follow his orders?

Fire with fire. The thoughts are mine but not mine. What does it mean?

As Azael's eyes drill into mine, I wonder if he's reading me? Communicating with me? What if he picks up on my absorption abilities? What if he realizes I'm his Achilles heel?

Fire with Fire? What does it mean? Use Margery's special ability against her maker? But if it didn't work against her… Hit him with my flame throwing mouth? Or maybe both.

My pause seems to piss him off because he bends forward and repeats, "Go… to… Margery." His loud roar tussles my hair.

When my legs turn according to Azael's will, I lift my palms, spit little flames onto them, and grunt through the pain. I aim up his man-skirt, a cross between a kilt and a Roman soldier's uniform, and rapid fire at the part I never ever want near Nita or any of the other Daughters of Light.

Direct hit.

Azael hops and grabs his crotch. It's enough of a distraction I'm able to blink and stumble backward, out of his control. Before he can draw me back in, I catch sight of Gorsky, diving at Azael's head, then out of arm's reach, over and over again.

I'm caught off guard, lifted into the air from behind, but breathe a sigh of relief as Trisha says into my ear, "Think you can latch onto him?"

"I'll try."

We ascend and she makes a wide turn. Below us, Gorsky continues to attack, shooting poison arrows at the fallen angel's chest, but my father's agile, blocking every shaft. Still, it's the distraction we need.

"Get ready." She throws me.

With arms spread wide, I prepare to latch onto a head three times the size of my own. Right on target, I come in for a landing on spikey hair that's like hugging a sharp metal security fence. I struggle to hold on for dear life, my hands barely covering his hypnotic eyes.

Trisha joins Gorsky, the two of them dive bombing Azael. Even blinded, he swats at each assault as if he can sense their presence. Then he connects with them both, and they sail out of sight, leaving me alone and clueless about what to do next. I squeeze my father's skull and wait for any sign I'm absorbing his sight, smell, taste, hearing… But he shows no decline, at least not physically. Are my absorption abilities working? After all, the process has been sporadic.

When he growls and reaches over his shoulder, I blow fire at his hand, inflicting a minor annoyance at best. Azael opens his arms at his sides and spins. Somehow, intuitively, I realize he's transforming into a twister to send me flying across the field. My legs extended outward while he jerks and bobs. All I can do is hold tighter and pray my shoulder blades don't dislocate. And there's still no indication Azael's forfeiting his powers. Maybe they were right to question my ability to complete this task.

No. I can do this.

Lightning flashes, the electrical surge triggering my palms to shoot cigarettes. I fly outward, groping at the air, legs flailing until a pine tree breaks my fall and fractures my spine. The whooshing tornado echoes in my head as I'm whacked by branch after branch until I reach the ground. Damn you, Trisha, for refusing to give me wings.

My vertebrae re-position in rapid succession. Within seconds, I jump to my feet and brush off pine needles with no residual aches and pains. Being able to heal in a fraction of my usual time must mean the absorption worked in at least one way.

A minute later, Trisha and Gorsky approach but loom in the distance.

"Well?" Trisha shouts over gusts of wind as she hedges closer.

"Well, what?" I stretch my arms overhead and shift side to side to test my spine.

She asks, "Did you absorb anything?"

"Healing faster!"

We turn toward my father's blusterous groans as his rotation decelerates. Black puffs of smoke escape from under his battle kilt as he's suspended midair, tweaking. Did a poison arrow penetrate his family jewels or was it something I did?

"Think you can mount Azael again?" Trisha, still hovering, reaches out to me. "Weaken him more?"

"He seems pretty weak!" I step backward, hands up, worried that latching onto my father in his condition could be catastrophic for us both. Of course, that would work to God's advantage.

"Any sense of what's happening?" she asks.

I shake my head.

We're hit with the smell of sulfur as a black veil engulfs Azael. Another bolt of lightning cracks, but this time a pitch-black, man-sized bird escapes the smokey cloud. Did my father shrink? No. It's one of Trisha's white warriors. I know it instinctively.

Trisha and Gorsky land beside me. She crosses her arms. "I can't believe this. It's—"

"A white warrior," I say, "trapped inside Azael's balls the day I was born."

She stares at me, wide-eyed. "But we didn't tell you about—"

"I must have absorbed the knowledge." I want to ask what else they've been keeping from me, but another crack of lightning releases a second black warrior.

"Oh, God." Trisha's mouth drops. "How many more could there be?"

"Ten." Again, I seem to know, as if they've been hiding in my own balls.

Trisha asks, "Any idea what happens when a white warrior incubates inside a fallen angel's testicles for over twenty years?"

"It's bad." I take a deep breath. "All bad."

Ten more rapid flashes later, they're all free.

As the smoke dissipates, it uncovers Azael, struggling to flap his wings. He falls, but the dozen black warriors catch him. Together, they ascend and soar in a dark streak to the north. Then, in a sonic boom, they disappear. But how much of my father was left behind... inside me?

Chapter 30

"**B**ARRY!" CANDY runs toward us, waving two bloody machetes. Her camouflage stretch pants and t-shirt are equally blood splattered. "What happened?" But there's no time to answer while she babbles a million words a minute, telling us about her skak and Minotaur count. When her eyes settle on Chump's headless body at the center of the clearing, she freezes and clams up.

"Where are the nuns? Is Pete alive?" Trisha asks. "Did you find Javier?"

"And Nita?" I butt in. "Don't forget about Nita."

Trisha flips me the bird. I reciprocate.

Candy squeals and points at Chump. She'll freak when she finds out I feasted on his brain. No way will she understand that I'd vomit every piece into his skull and submit to any sort of magic to bring him back.

"I know, he's gone. He's a substantial loss." Trisha pats Candy's back, consoling her without blaming me, at least for now. She goes on to say, "Azael got away, so this isn't over."

"No, it's not." I point at the tree line—sets of red and yellow and orange glowing eyes pop into view. Their evil growls amplify and branches snap as they close in. "Skaks and Minotaurs and hellhounds."

"Oh my," Candy adds, then stiffens her back. "Pete and the nuns! They're in the middle of that." She takes off, kicking up sand, her machetes presented at neck level. Trisha and Gorsky follow skyward, a breeze from their flapping wings brushing my face.

The switchblade, my only weapon, won't do in this battle, so I retrieve

Chump's ax and rush to catch up. But just as quickly as Margery's army appeared, the eyeballs flicker and disappear. They seem in full retreat, their rumbling footsteps lost in the distance.

"What the hell." I slow to a walk and pause beside Candy, our weapons limp at our sides.

"Well, that was anticlimactic," she says. "Not that I'm complaining. Smells like there were a lot of hellhounds and Minotaurs ready to attack." Candy sniffs the air, then turns her nose me. "Or is that you?"

"Ha, ha."

Trisha flies in for a landing and says, "You think they ran away from Barry?"

"Wouldn't that be special, a hellhound afraid of me?" I'm flooded with memories of the beast that bit through my neck. I'd love the opportunity to bite him back.

Candy moves in closer and continues to sniff at me. "You feeling dark and horney, because you reek like Azael?"

"Stop it!" I shrug and step away while smelling the collar on my t-shirt. What a nightmare if I absorbed his scent.

"Well, you don't look any different." Candy walks around me. "But you sure do smell… nasty."

"It's from being so close to him. It's in my clothes."

"Let's hope so." Trisha closes in to sniff my shoulder, then shivers. "I don't get what attracts human women to that mix of sulfur and men's locker room stench."

"That's not what I smell." Candy smiles and winks at me.

Ew.

In need of a distraction, I say, "Don't we have people to locate and demons to dismember?" With skill and purpose, I twirl the ax like Chump would. A reminder his knowledge and skills are now mine. While holding the weapon at the ready, I'm confident that it'll soon be buried in Margery's head. But only if she didn't flee with the others.

"This way." Candy darts to the right and moves deeper into the tree line. I follow her bouncing ass, assuming her intuition is leading the way. An incentive not to bite it again. Trisha returns to the sky.

A few minutes later, Candy stops and points toward drifting sparks and a gruff voice, barking orders in the distance. Margery's in human form, which is no less threatening than her ten-foot demon stance.

Behind a tree with the cold ax against my cheek, I wonder how many skaks are with her and where they might be. We could already be surrounded. Hopefully, Trisha and Gorsky are hovering nearby and ready to dive in to decimate the area.

"Bar-ry," Margery says in a slow singsong.

The forest goes silent except for a breeze swooshing through trees. My hands heat up, the cigarettes seeming to know they are near their original host. Then my whole body quivers, but not out of fear. All I want is to bury the ax into her sparky troll-doll head and give her a permanent part.

I peek around the tree and see at least ten of the little mummy bastards, hunched over and staring our direction. None appear to have weapons, but why would they? Their mouths are full of tiger fish teeth. Just the thought provokes an aching in my leg, where the one bit me a few days ago.

Pops pop pop sound from above. Gorsky swoops in, shooting the crossbow like a machine gun, taking out a few skaks with his terrible aim. Candy joins the battle, slashing her machetes through shriveled mummies and seeming to speak in tongues.

I follow a path toward Margery, who first stands her ground. When our eyes meet, her head tilts, as if she's examining the new me: part Barry, part Chump, part Azael… and part her. For once, she seems confused while sidestepping left, then right, then left. She points and yells, "Get him, morons! Get Barry! Restrain him!" But the skaks are an aimless swarm, so she runs scared.

"Oh no you don't!" I lift the ax, take aim, and hurl it at her back. With ease, it sails through the air and engages between her shoulder blades. "Thank you, Chump."

But Margery holds her ground. No doubt her remaining fight is transforming her into ten feet of demon madness.

"Candy! Machete!" I yell.

She's fifteen feet to my right with half a dozen skaks between us. "Catch!" She throws one, up high, in my direction.

With wide eyes, I stiffen, thinking about how catching a ball is a challenge. *Chump, don't fail me now.* And he doesn't. It's an easy catch. And when I realize every ounce of fear I once had for Margery is gone, I thank Azael.

Margery's a foot taller as I swipe the machete across her wrinkled neck. Her head launches; the sparks in her hair snuff into a few puffs of smoke. Margery falls like timber, and her head bounces like a ball until it reverses direction, rolling toward her shoulders. I snatch it by the hair before she can merge back together.

Her voice gurgles as she says, "Loser. You are *so* dead!" The breeze blows a gust of her sour tobacco and rotten meat halitosis into my face.

I hold my breath and show her the destruction. "Look around and tell me who's the loser?"

"Ha!" She spits blood. "I lost a few skaks, but Azael got away from you."

A burp builds in my gut and burns into my esophagus. "Fuck you!" The words release with flames across her puckered face. I laugh and cough up smoke.

When something tugs at my pants, I glance down to find Margery clutching my jeans. So I chop off her hand, a stupid move because it's free to climb my leg. I stomp, trying to free its grip, but the fingers are fast with a tight hold.

"Candy!" I hop around. "A little help here!"

"Kinda busy… covering *your* ass!" she says between swipes across dry crunchy skaks' necks.

Pete and the nuns join in, further clearing the area of multiplying skaks. I cry for him to help as the hand fumbles around my knee.

"Fighting skaks," he says. "Can't reach you."

Margery hisses and lashes her snake-like tongue around my neck. I choke and gasp for air. But nearby, the battle continues, no one noticing her strangle hold. As her hand reaches my crotch and crushes my balls, I scream like a five-year-old girl and release the machete. All I can do is grope at my crotch, trying to open her fingers.

What to do?

I drop to my knees, unable to breathe.

The switchblade.

I reach into my pocket, pull out the knife Chump gave me, snap the blade to attention, and slash at her tongue. The snaky lasso separates from her head and releases my neck, but it stretches midair and reaches to return to her mouth. I whack it with the switchblade, and it falls to the ground. But she tightens her grip, and her tongue slithers up my leg to join the assault.

With Margery's head in one hand and the knife in the other, I insanely contemplate stabbing at my crotch. Instead, I call out, "Candy! Please!"

This time, she responds, but her first impulse is to convulse with laughter. "How did you manage—"

"Shut up and take her head. Get the tongue." Both better options than letting Candy anywhere near my balls.

She takes Margery by the hair and holds her at arm's length. "Oh, what I'd like to do to you…"

Oh, how I'd love to see what she does too, but only after Margery releases her hand, and I've chopped it into a million pieces.

Trisha lands, and I point and beg, "Do something."

She looks at my crotch and covers her mouth.

Through gritted teeth, I say, "Help me!"

"Alright, although I'm enjoying this more than dropping you on your head." Trisha squats and taps a red-polished index fingernail on

Margery's hand. It drops to the ground. I fall to the side, eyes closed, clutching my family jewels. She pokes me with her Stiletto. "Get up."

When I open my eyes, I'm staring into the mouth of a decapitated skak, still chomping at the air. It's incentive enough to jump to my feet. Again, the rapid healing leaves me feeling no pain. I hop around, repeating, "I'm perfect."

"You… perfect? Pshaw." Candy says.

I flip her the bird and look around. With their leader headless, the skaks are fleeing by the dozens, a few of the nuns and Pete in pursuit.

"Anyone locate Nita?" I ask.

"Here we go again with that girl," Trisha says.

"Can't you use Azael's Romeo abilities to sniff her out?" Candy slaps her thigh and laughs.

"She's over there, tied to a tree," Trisha says.

"Did you find Javier?" Candy asks.

I don't stick around to hear the answer. Nita needs me.

Chapter 31

"NITA!" I zigzag through a cluster of aspen trees toward a muffled voice.

"To the right," Trisha calls in the distance.

A few seconds later our eyes meet. She's on the ground, tied to a tree, moonlight reflecting off the tears on her cheeks. Her wings are torn off and stacked beside her.

"Oh, God! What did Margery do to you?" I rush to Nita, untie her pale wrists, and think how I'll never get used to her being a white warrior, wings or no wings. She yanks at the twine, helping to loosen the binding, then jumps to her feet and wraps her arms around me. I lean over and kiss her forehead.

Trisha joins us. "Don't touch her!"

I throw up my hands, but Nita's hug tightens.

"Stop." Trisha pulls us apart. "We have no idea what you'll absorb from a mix of human and demon."

"C'mon. This is not the first time I've touched her, and nothing's happened so far." I lower my arms.

"Like when you kissed me—"

"Bear, you kissed her?" She steps backward.

"It meant nothing," I say.

"You're just jealous." Nita tells Trisha, then puffs out her bottom lip. The two move closer and face off.

Trisha rolls her eyes. "We have bigger problems than who is jealous of whom."

"Nita." I point at a cluster of nuns, hoping to distract her. "I chopped off Margery's head. She's over there."

She turns, follows my finger, and squeals as she runs away.

"C'mon," I tell Trisha, "Margery ripped off her wings. She deserves a little sympathy."

"Maybe if she had also torn off Nita's arms and legs."

"You call yourself an angel apprentice?"

As Trisha and I progress toward the nuns, she continues to lecture, "We have to figure out where Azael is headed. And who knows if God will let you finish absorbing him? Not to mention figuring out what you absorbed in the first place. But priority number one is cleaning up this mess and burying Margery's body parts across the mountains."

When we approach the scene of the dismemberment, Nita's wielding an ax overhead, taking aim, and Candy's holding the demon bitch's head up to watch. Everyone steps back. With intent and brute force, she swings downward like a lumberjack on a quota. With her first chop, she screams, "Disgusting savage!" With subsequent strikes, she says things that make the nuns blush. This is the best possible way to incapacitate Margery.

Black blood splatters across the ground and on anyone nearby, then the fluid animates, intent on returning to its source along with the rest of the chunks of demon flesh. The sisters groan and cover their noses with veils to protect against the harsh odor.

"Nice job." I reach for the ax, grasping the handle. Chump's absorbed expertise warns that Nita may be inflicting her revenge, but a demon chopped into dozens of pieces will take much longer to pack into burlap sacks.

"Everyone, grab a bag," Pete says while he rejoins us. "Start stuffing."

Before Margery can reassemble, we're quick to comply, except for Nita, who drops to her knees to catch her breath and cry. It's good to see her human side, which makes me want to reach out to hug her and tell her Margery will never hurt anyone again. But I don't dare cross Trisha as she steps between us.

In the background, the nuns take over, tying the bags while the rest of us regroup.

"Did you… get him?" Nita asks. "Is Azael eliminated?"

"Partially absorbed. Not eliminated," I say. "He got away."

"What does partially absorbed mean?" Nita asks.

"We don't know yet," Pete says, "but Barry was able to weaken Azael."

Candy approaches Nita. "Did you see Javier? Did Margery say where he is?"

"Yes." Nita perks up. "Margery buried him in the sand to make him a skak."

"She what?" Candy asks.

"The courier plots are this way." Trisha treks across the unstable forest floor in heels, as steady as can be, and we follow.

We exit the trees and rush beyond the clearing to a sandy area on the opposite side. There are over a dozen grave-size holes with piles of sand beside them. Shovels lay on the ground or are stuck upright in the sand. The Minotaurs who were unearthing skaks abandoned the site in a hurry, likely after the nuns attacked.

"Could Javier be in one of these?" I point at a few graves with loose sand piled high.

"Barry, you're useful for a change." Candy grabs a shovel and rushes to a fresh mound. "He's in here."

"How do you know?" I ask.

"I have a feeling." She starts digging.

I help. Her hunches have been right so far, especially about me getting into trouble. The deeper we shovel, the more sulfur and rotten meat overpowers the air, a reminder that skaks are made from a mixture of Margery's and a hellhound's spit. Poor guy had to endure a shower of both.

Four feet down, we hit something. I step aside as Candy pulls Javier's limp body from the pit. His skin hasn't shriveled, possibly a good sign. She slaps his face. "Wake up. Please, wake up." But he remains lifeless.

"Is he dead?" I ask.

She checks his neck for a pulse. "No. Alive. But he needs Ulla and Inez. Now!"

"Gorsky!" Trisha calls out. Within seconds her only remaining white warrior flies in for a landing. "Bring Javier to the cave."

He nods, wraps his arms under Javier's armpits, and takes to the night sky. Hopefully, the two-headed lady has learned enough about my skak bite to undo any transition he may have gone through.

"Let me go with them," Candy says.

"No," Trisha says. "This area needs to be cleared of skaks before morning. That includes unearthing these other graves and decapitating the remaining couriers in transition, although a few of the ones recently buried might be worthy of turning into white warriors."

"Thought you didn't want me to touch anyone," I say.

"Nice try." Trisha narrows in on me with a lifted eyebrow. "Digging a hole doesn't require touching anyone."

"Damn." I pick up my shovel and get to work. The sooner this job is done, the better.

Then Pete approaches in a hurry, arms flailing, as if Boss is in charge.

"What now?" Trisha huffs and crosses her arms.

"We can't find Margery's tongue."

"Oh, hell." I stop mid-scoop. "I dropped it when her hand was on my nuts. I told Candy—"

"Sure, blame me," she says.

"Shut up!" Trisha says. "Everyone, drop what you're doing! Locate that tongue!"

Chapter 32

Y THE next morning, we've cleaned up the mess at the sand dunes, but Margery's tongue is still on the loose. At least Trisha and Gorsky buried her other body parts in undisclosed locations throughout the Sangre De Cristo Mountains. It would take her tongue a couple centuries to slither across the mountain range to find her other pieces. Then again, Margery's minions and my father are still out there, somewhere.

Except for Chump, we're all alive, gathering at the sight of the sunken boarding house. He's zipped inside a black body bag at the base of the only tree. Well, except for his brain matter, continuing to digest in my gut. We're preparing for Chump's funeral, and the day matches our collective mood: dark, dreary, and rainy.

"It's time," Pete says as we all join together. "Time to say goodbye, get this pit closed, and move on with our lives… our mission… up north in Denver."

"None of this should have happened." A red-faced Candy turns to me. "I can't believe you ate Chumps brain."

I hang my head to avoid eye contact.

"It's time for action, not judgment," Pete says. "Stay focused. Chump would want it that way."

"Agreed," Javier pats Candy's back. "C'mon. I'll help you get Chump in the hole."

"I can do it." She pulls away, grabs the body bag, and raises it overhead like a power lifter. Two seconds later, Chump's airborne, headed for the same cavity we pulled Ulla and Inez from the day the boarding house sunk.

Ulla and Inez approach, a small cloth bag in hand that's filled with a concoction meant to close the hole. Or, as was explained by Pete, merge everything into a giant blob, although he wouldn't admit to what was in the house that may need permanent destruction. Why would he? Since absorbing an undetermined amount of a fallen angel, I'm untrustworthy. It's like I have a plague.

Inez shouts, "Surround hole!"

The nuns follow Sister Theresa to the far end of the lot; we unholy types form the rest of the circle.

"A moment of silence before we close this chapter of our lives." Pete slumps and slides fingers into his jean's pockets.

"No sniveling." Javier squints and wipes an eye. "Chump wouldn't want it." When he speaks, he exposes pointy teeth, the only side-effect that remains from his skak transition.

While everyone bows their heads, my brain churns with acquired knowledge: angels, demons, weapons, topography, torture, omens, and more. Worst of all, I'm fighting an urge to run off and locate Azael, unsure if I'd finish the absorption or conquer the world with him. A fact I'm reluctant to admit to anyone around the circle.

Pete breaks the silence. "Chump lived at the hotel, but he loved this house. He'd appreciate being laid to rest here." Interesting choice of words, considering there's no rest for dead couriers. He's either guarding Hell's refugee camp or counting souls in Purgatory.

The two-headed lady hands the pouch to Trisha, prompting her to fly above the pit and sprinkle the contents of the bag over the wreckage. We step back as the earth and house creak and churn. Boards and shingles stir like a boiling pot of noodles. Seconds later, the land returns to a natural state: dry grass, tumbleweed, rocks, and a new tree marking Chump's grave. Wild sunflower bloom, toping it all off.

Then it hits me hard. Chump is gone. The only one who fought for me, protected me, didn't fear me. Everyone around the circle deems me a threat, even more so now that I've proven my worth. They would have put me in a cage or mountain tomb if God hadn't decided I deserved a chance to finish off Azael.

Javier approaches and holds out a bottle of whiskey.

"Thanks." I grab it, lift the bottle in cheers, and take a swig. "We should have thrown a bottle in before the hole filled."

"Oh, I've got him covered," Javier says. "There are three bottles in the bag with him."

"Good thinking." I chug some more, hogging the whiskey near my chest.

"Gimme some of that." Candy snatches the bottle and liquid splashes onto her hand. She licks it off.

"Get your fill," Trisha says as she lands. "We're headed to Margery's Trinidad Warehouse."

Candy chokes on a swig.

"Why?" I ask. "Don't tell me we have to clean up that place too."

"We're transporting the unused evil energy canisters back to Denver."

"We're what?" Candy asks.

"You heard her," Pete says. "We can't leave evil energy lying around. Satan could send another demon to try to restart the operation to open the Gates of Hell. We need the warehouse in Trinidad inoperable, and Javier has volunteered to stay behind to keep the place closed.

Trisha adds, "You and Barry will drive one of the OTG vans and the nuns will drive the others."

"Have you considered how pissed the CEO of Hell will be when he finds out we've stolen his evil energy?" I ask. "We do this and my warrant for damnation will end up with another ten pages for additional charges."

"For once, I'm with Barry," Candy says. "How do you expect us to reach Denver in one piece in an OTG van?"

"Besides Gorsky and Nita, I've turned a dozen of the couriers we unearthed into white warriors," Trisha says.

"This is bullshit," Candy says while bobbing her head.

"Yes, it is, but so is my life," I say. "Let's just get this over with."

About the Author

Winnie Jean Howard (a.k.a Mean Winnie Jean) writes dark humor for all ages. Her main focus is creating action-packed stories that are quick reads.

While born in Chicago, today she lives near Denver, Colorado with her ever growing family. She enjoys hiking with her husband and beagle, drinks way too much wine, and watches way too many zombie movies. In fact, she's a bit addicted to any form of media that aims to scare.

For over thirty years, she's been an IT geek, professional writer, and artist. She's also been involved in the development of anything from simple websites to network monitoring to space defense systems. Recently, she returned to school to add graphic designer to her list of careers. Besides fiction, she writes technical specifications, instructional manual, marketing articles, organizational newsletters, and much more. She's also the founder, Chief Editor and Creative Director over at ArmLin House Productions.

More About the Author
winniejeanhoward.com
facebook.com/winniejeanhoward
instagram.com/meanwinniejean
deviantart.com/meanwinniejean
tiktok.com/@meanwinniejean

About the Publisher

ArmLin House is a unique publisher and production company. We help you develop your story in a memoir, business book, instructional video, and more. Then we format your story and help you present your work, whether you release it yourself or we do it for you. And once your story is out there, we can help you promote it with written and visual aids.

It's our mission to help our clients succeed in whatever they do. We take your visions and make them possible through coaching and distribution assistance. The products we help produce are informational and entertaining, as well as help you market yourself and your business. We produce based on your needs, whether it be in print, digital, audio, or video formats. Then we help release it to a worldwide audience. .

Contact the Publisher
armlinhouse.com
facebook.com/armlinhouse
instagram/armlinhouse